She stopped, turned to find Joseph leaning against a porch pillar, watching her. This time her shiver had nothing to do with anger. She remembered how it had felt to rest her head against his broad shoulder, remembered what it was like to feel secure, safe.

Only to have him push her away. He'd wanted her to shelve her career and become the kind of wife she'd vowed never to be.

A cop's wife—giving up *her* career to make *him* happy.

And yet the attraction between them had sizzled.

"Can we talk?" he asked. "About us."

"That's not even a topic," she said. "There is no us."

His jaw clenched. "We have to work together. Without letting our past interfere. Can we do that?"

"We can try."

He reached to grasp her hand in a handshake, and the tingles that danced up her arm told her she was in trouble.

Books by Lynette Eason

Love Inspired Suspense

Lethal Deception
River of Secrets
Holiday Illusion
A Silent Terror
A Silent Fury

LYNETTE EASON

grew up in Greenville, SC. Her home church, Northgate Baptist, had a tremendous influence on her during her early years. She credits Christian parents and dedicated Sunday School teachers for her acceptance of Christ at the tender age of eight. Even as a young girl, she knew she wanted her life to reflect the love of Jesus.

Lynette attended the University of South Carolina in Columbia, SC, then moved to Spartanburg, SC, to attend Converse College, where she obtained her master's degree in education. During this time, she met the boy next door, Jack Eason—and married him. Jack is the Executive Director of the Sound of Light Ministries. Lynette and Jack have two precious children, Lauryn, eight years old, and Will, who is six. She and Jack are members of New Life Baptist Fellowship Church in Boiling Springs, SC, where Jack serves as the worship leader and Lynette teaches Sunday School to the four- and five-year-olds.

A SILENT FURY

LYNETTE EASON

Steeple
Hill®

Published by Steeple Hill Books™

STEEPLE HILL BOOKS

Steeple
Hill®

Recycling programs
for this product may
not exist in your area.

ISBN-13: 978-0-373-44354-3

A SILENT FURY

www.SteepleHill.com

Printed in U.S.A.

Refrain from anger and turn from wrath; do not fret—it leads only to evil. For evil men will be cut off, but those who hope in the Lord will inherit the land.

—*Psalms* 37:8–9

As always, to Jesus Christ.
You are as good as your Word.

Thanks go out to

My agent! Tamela, you rock. Thank you for your
unwavering support and belief in my writing.
God bless you!

Thanks to Officer Jim Hall with the ACFW Carolina
Christian Writers group for getting all my cop stuff
right. And if something's *not* right, it's my fault!

And once again, I thank my family and friends
for their encouragement and love as I write for the
One who gives me the stories.

ONE

Pack it up, Santino, you've got a murderer and a missing girl to find. His boss's words echoed in his mind as Joseph Santino, Special Agent for the FBI, watched the Greenville-Spartanburg International Airport spread out in tiny detail below him. He'd been fine with the assignment until the man had added, "Oh, and you'll be partnering up with a homicide detective there." He looked down at his papers. "Catelyn Clark."

At that point, Joseph wasn't fine anymore. In fact, he'd done everything to get out of going, short of quitting his job. None of his arguments worked. So, here he was mentally preparing himself to face the one woman he'd never gotten over. The one woman he'd vowed to banish from his thoughts—and failed.

The plane landed, and Joseph grabbed his carry-on, anxious to get this case started so he could get it finished and get back to New York.

An hour and a half later he found himself staring down at the face of a sixteen-year-old girl laid out on the slab in the morgue.

Victim: Tracy Merritt.
Cause of death: blunt-force trauma to the back of the head.

The murder weapon: unknown and still missing.
The suspect: Dylan Carlisle.

Best friend to Joseph's seventeen-year-old brother, Alonso.
Only the police hadn't arrested Dylan because they didn't
have enough evidence. Yet. Joseph's job was to find Kelly
Franklin, the dead girl's best friend who'd been reported
missing the day Tracy's body had been found. It was suspected
that they'd been together and Kelly had been forcibly removed
from the scene. Most likely, by the killer.

What a mess. Joseph sighed and turned away shaking his
head.

His buddy, Victor Shields, captain of criminal investigations
within the local police department, willingly offered Joseph his
services and resources. Joseph had been a uniformed cop under
Victor's leadership before moving to the FBI. About a year
after working in New York, Victor had called him for help.
Joseph had responded and found the man's runaway teenage
daughter, bringing her home safely.

Now, business brought Joseph home once again. Only this
time, the missing person hit close to home. A student at the
Palmetto Deaf School, Kelly was not only Dylan's girlfriend,
but she was also a friend of Alonso, Joseph's deaf brother.

Joseph's heart tightened as he thought about his family.
Having a deaf brother, mother and sister, Joseph, the eldest of
six siblings, had grown up as the protector of the clan. Active
in the deaf community, knowledgeable about the tight, small
world within their own culture, Joseph knew he was the perfect
person for this job. Because he was accepted as part of the deaf
world, he could ask questions and get answers where other
hearing cops couldn't. At least not in a timely manner. And with
one girl dead and another missing, time was of the essence.

He looked up at Kip Kennedy, the medical examiner, a

balding man in his late fifties Joseph had known from his beat cop days. "I'm going to find out who did this to her."

Kip sighed, shook his head. "I don't know what this world is coming to. Kids dying, teenagers being snatched. It ain't right. Unfortunately, the killer didn't leave his calling card."

"I want to know everything you find on this girl. I don't care if you think it's not important. Okay?"

"Sure. I'll give you everything. I promise." He looked down at the girl who'd never smile, never grow up, never have her own family. "It's the least she deserves, and I'll do my best to give you the tools to find the one who did this to her."

Dead kids tied him in knots. Joseph did his best to shut down emotion and focus on the facts. "Thanks, Kip. I appreciate it."

A young woman in her mid-twenties popped her head in the door. "The Merritt family is here."

Kip nodded, looked up at Joseph and grimaced, his bald head shining in the overhead fluorescent light. "This is the part I really hate."

"Yeah."

Grabbing a lightweight jacket, Detective Catelyn Clark headed back to the Palmetto Deaf School. Tracy Merritt's body had already been removed from the campus and taken to the morgue. As a homicide detective with the Spartanburg police force, Catelyn had been one of the first on the scene. She'd watched the crime-scene investigators do their job and had pitched in where she could. They'd found a baseball jacket and a flip-flop among other things that may or may not be related to the case. The flip-flop had been identified as belonging to Kelly Franklin, the missing girl.

But still, she wanted to go over the scene one more time. Before the yellow tape was removed and the school went back to normal. Her partner, Ethan O'Hara, was away on vacation with his bride of one year. He'd return home tomorrow, but would still have a couple of days off before returning to work. He'd spend them with his wife, Marianna. The man was so happy, it was disgusting. And incredibly sweet. Longing rose up in her, and she immediately vanquished it.

Only one man had ever tempted her to think about the possibility of matrimony, and she'd gotten burned as a result. Two years ago Joseph Santino had been on the verge of asking her to marry him—and she'd been so close to throwing caution to the wind and saying yes. Then she'd found out his true expectations of what he felt a wife should be and she'd shoved him away with both hands—and he'd left, moved to another state. Which was just as well, she reminded herself. Joseph's actions had simply reinforced a decision she'd made long ago. She would never marry another officer—tempted though she might have been once upon a time.

Because if there was one thing she was sure about in this life, it was the fact that two cops married to each other simply created a war zone.

Her parents had certainly taught her that.

And why she was even thinking along those lines puzzled her. It must be because her boss had told her who she'd be working this case with: Joseph Santino. Groaning in frustration at her inability to shove her resurrected thoughts about that man from her mind, she desperately focused on the task before her. Find who killed Tracy Merritt and arrest the creep.

Period.

Pulling into the gate, she flashed her badge at security. This school had seen a lot of police action lately. Just a little over a year ago, teacher Marianna O'Hara, Joseph's deaf sister, had been held hostage in her classroom by a power hungry politician. Thankfully, that situation had ended peacefully.

And now this.

Briefly, Catelyn wondered if she should remove herself from the case. Being the ex-girlfriend of the main FBI agent called in to assist with the case might cause a few raised eyebrows—if they knew.

But that was the past.

She'd worry about him later.

Now, she turned her thoughts to the young man who was the main suspect in the case: Dylan Carlisle. A hotheaded teen who convincingly protested his innocence.

Yeah, right. She'd been up that road before, had the scar to prove it and wasn't buying it this time around.

Dylan hadn't been arrested yet, but if the evidence continued to build, she'd have him in jail so fast his head would spin, convincing protests notwithstanding.

At the crime scene, she pulled to a stop and stepped out of the car. The scene had been cleared by the authorities, but not yet cleaned up. Good. She'd have a chance to go over it one more time.

The lone figure standing inside the yellow tape made her pull up and stare. He couldn't be here already. Surely not. The figure turned and met her gaze.

Yep, it was him.

Sucking in a deep breath, she blew it out slowly, telling herself to calm down. Praying her voice didn't shake at the sudden shock of seeing him, she said, "Hello, Joseph."

Joseph stared. He couldn't help it. It had been two years since he'd seen Catelyn. Even though he'd returned home to visit family during that time, he'd never run into her. She'd made herself scarce during his visits in spite of the fact that she'd stayed friends with his sister Alissa.

But he'd thought about her. Thought about calling, finding her, asking her to clarify what went wrong with their relationship. And each time he thought about it, he pushed the feelings aside, not wanting to put himself back in a place where he could be hurt again. And she *had* hurt him because she'd seemed to walk away from him without ever making her reasons clear. At the time, he'd been furious with her, confused and pained by her actions—and, he admitted to himself, prideful. So he'd let her have her space and time passed.

But he'd missed her. She'd practically grown up in his house and Joseph had loved her since she'd been a teenager with a chip on her shoulder. She'd fit right in with his family, six brothers and sisters, his mom and dad and a grandmother.

Catelyn had adopted them all and learned the language they'd used most around the house: ASL, American Sign Language.

And now she was even prettier than he remembered. With a glint in her eye that said she wasn't happy to see him.

Well, too bad. He was here to stay until the end. No matter what it took to find Kelly and put Tracy's killer behind bars. Even if it meant dealing with Catelyn and old feelings that had never truly died.

"Hello, Catie."

"Don't call me that. My name's Catelyn."

Nope, she hadn't changed a bit. Just as contrary as she ever was. "Fine," he clipped. "*Catelyn,* what do you think about this case so far? Any new leads on Kelly or Tracy?"

Compassion softened her gaze for a moment. "No, nothing yet. Kelly's poor family, they're beside themselves. And her brother, Billy…" She shook her head. "He's having a hard time. They go to my church and I've known them awhile. You never had a chance to meet them as they came after you left."

He ignored her dig. She'd been the one to send him on his way. His gaze swept the scene again as he wondered how to respond. Then decided not to.

In spite of the fact that the scene had been cleared, he'd

slipped blue crime-scene booties over his shoes so as not to disturb anything in the area. He couldn't help it. He simply couldn't walk a crime scene without them. He watched as Catelyn went ahead and slipped a pair over her shoes. Apparently she felt the same way.

Attention to detail.

Notice everything; mentally record the scene to pull up later. And write everything down. Good notes were essential. He had no doubt Catelyn's would be unquestionably precise and detailed.

"Dylan's jacket was found there," she offered.

"Where?" Joseph's head snapped up. Victor hadn't mentioned anything about a jacket.

She scraped a hand through that silky blond mane that never seemed to stay where she wanted it. He remembered smoothing it down, around her cheeks, his fingers grazing skin so soft, he…

Clearing his throat, he asked, "What was his jacket doing at the crime scene? He doesn't even go to this school anymore now that he's playing baseball with Esterman High."

"I know. We pulled him in for questioning and he claims he met Kelly here, they were walking, she was cold and he gave her his jacket."

"So how did it wind up on the ground?" He pointed to the marker indicating where the jacket had been found.

"He says he has no idea. That he left his jacket with her and he was going to come back to get it the next day, which would be today. Tracy was found last night. We still haven't heard anything from Kelly."

"You don't believe him." Joseph stated it as fact, his eyes never leaving her face. If he hadn't been studying her so intently, he would have missed the brief flicker of regret.

She shrugged, turning back to assess the scene. He wondered

if she was just avoiding looking at him. She said, "I don't know, Joseph. And that's the truth. I don't want to think Dylan capable of something like this. Dylan's aunt is a dispatcher with the department. His mom is a single mother and while his dad's in the picture, he's not around much. Dylan's track record isn't great, and kids do stupid stuff all the time that turns deadly." Another shrug. "Who knows? I'm reserving judgment until all the evidence is in."

"Alonso sent me a text message. Dylan's a good friend of his, of our family. Alonso firmly believes in his buddy's innocence and is begging me to prove it." He blew out a sigh and looked at her. "You've already got him tried and found guilty, haven't you?"

"No." Her eyes got that glint again, the one that said he was walking a fine line, and she was having trouble holding on to her temper. Not for the first time he thought she should have been a redhead. "I didn't say that. I said I'm following the evidence."

"And what if that evidence is all circumstantial and yet still leads back to Dylan?"

"Then I'll arrest him."

Catelyn hated the tension between the two of them. Once upon a time, Joseph had been her best friend, her confidante, the only man who'd ever made her seriously think about tossing away her personal rule about never marrying a cop. She turned away from him, walked to the edge of the tape.

His voice came from her right. "What else did they find?"

"A ring with some blood on it." She kept her words clipped, professional.

"The girl's or someone else's?"

"Don't know yet. It just went into the lab. You know how fast the turnaround time is." Sarcasm dripped off the words.

Joseph snorted. "Yeah."

Catelyn came closer, asking the question she'd wondered for the last couple of years—ever since he'd left. "So, how have you been?"

"Good. Just working a lot. New York's a fascinating city."

"I'm sure." Now she was stuck. Backed into that awkward conversational corner, silence stretching, making her itch to escape.

Joseph walked the perimeter, just inside the tape. Bending down, he touched the grass. "There was some kind of scuffle here. The grass is really torn up in this spot. I mean, I know it's a school with kids everywhere, but this area's kind of off the beaten path."

Relieved to be back on a safe topic, she said, "Yes, the crime-scene guys looked it over, got the pictures. No prints, though. The ground's too hard."

Glancing at the sky, Joseph lamented, "Could have used the rain that's coming this afternoon a couple of days ago."

She walked a few feet outside the tape. Several strategically placed large boulders lined the curving entrance to the school. More were placed under the shade trees near the pasture where students like to gather in the afternoon. Catelyn scanned them and something caught her attention. She leaned down, pulling the small high-powered digital camera from her pocket. She snapped two pictures of the item, then pulled out a glove. Just because something turned up outside the tape, didn't mean it wasn't evidence. With a steady hand, she picked it up.

Wood. About two inches wide by six inches long.

Looking around, she spied the trees, a wooden play set off to the left, wooden cedar chips had been spread near the horse pasture. The wooden fence. Wood everywhere. Carefully, she studied the piece. Scanned the wood surrounding her once more. It didn't really match anything nearby. Possibly the light, wooden play set.

So what was it?

"What have you got?"

"I was just trying to figure that out. It's a piece of wood, but I don't know what kind or where it came from. There's nothing else around here like it. See, it's smooth on this side, but rough around the edges and underneath."

He came closer, stood next to her to inspect the piece. She shivered at the proximity and had to concentrate on his words so she wouldn't think how wonderful it felt to have him near again. He was saying, "Could be part of that play set. They just built it."

"It's probably nothing, but…" Catelyn snagged a plastic bag from her pocket, one she'd stuck in there just in case. She dropped the piece into it and moved a couple of inches away. She couldn't breathe with him that close. It galled her he could still stir her up when she just wanted to forget the anger and hurt he'd left her with two years ago. "I'll just get this over to the lab. They'll be able to tell us what kind of wood it is."

"Sometime in this century, I hope." He sounded jaded, resigned.

"Ah!"

The guttural cry brought them both around. Alonso, Joseph's brother stood there with Dylan Carlisle. Joseph took note of Dylan's clenched fists, ragged breathing and air of desperation. Seeing he had their attention, he signed, "I didn't do it. I didn't kill Tracy!"

TWO

Joseph strode to his brother and the distraught young man. He gripped Dylan's shoulders and squeezed, hoping to transmit understanding and comfort. Dropping his hands, he signed, "We're going to find out who did."

Alonso shifted, anxiety oozing from him. Joseph had sent a text message to his brother to let him know that he had arrived in town and would see him soon, but after his visit to the morgue, Joseph had come straight to the crime scene.

Alonso and Dylan had come to find him. He studied the lanky young suspect in front of him. Frantic blue eyes, blond hair, a smattering of freckles across a sharp nose and pale cheeks. Then Alonso, who was Dylan's physical opposite. A little shorter with brown eyes and dark skin, he was a younger version of Joseph, their Italian heritage prominently displayed.

A small cut on Dylan's chin looked angry, red. Alonso had a bit of stubble that had already grown out since this morning. His little brother and his friends were already shaving, growing up. *Were* grown up, he realized. Dylan was considered a man and old enough to be tried as an adult if convicted of murder. What would that do to Alonso who fervently believed in his friend's innocence?

Joseph signed, "I believe you. Unless I find solid evidence to the contrary, I believe you. Okay?"

Chest still heaving, Dylan glared back at Joseph, and Joseph flinched at the agony in the boy's eyes. Either the kid was an excellent actor or he was telling the truth.

Catelyn came up to sign, "You two shouldn't be here."

Joseph wanted to tell her to stay away, but she was right, neither of the teens should be here. Wrapping one arm around his brother's shoulder, and the other around Dylan, he steered them back to the idling vehicle Alonso had left in the middle of the road. With his free hand, Joseph signed, "Let's go home. Catelyn will take care of this."

Dylan shot Catelyn one last glare that gradually turned pleading. "Please believe me."

Compassion flickered briefly before her expression solidified into granite. "I'll believe the evidence."

This time Joseph shot her a hard look as he turned the boys toward the car once more. Joseph signed and spoke to his brother, "You two go to the house. I'll follow you there and we'll talk, all right?"

"Wait a minute," Catelyn protested, "this is my case, too. If you're going to question him, I need to be there."

Joseph turned back to look at her, his breath hissing from his lungs. Even driving him crazy, even in the midst of a murder investigation and, yes, even exhibiting her bulldog tenacity, she still had the power to stop him in his tracks with her beauty. He really had to get over that. She'd made it clear she didn't want anything to do—romantically—with him.

Hands on her hips, feet planted wide, she thrust her jaw forward and narrowed her eyes. Arguing with her would be fruitless.

Besides, she was right. They were there to work together. They both had a common goal. Find the bad guy. He had to put aside his personal feelings and keep his heart under control. "I'm not questioning them in any official capacity right now.

I'm just talking to my brother and his friend." He paused. "But, all right, come on. I'm staying with my parents right now, so why don't you meet us there?"

Shock at easy acquiescence flashed across her features before she could cover it up. But she didn't hesitate. "Right, see you there."

During the ten-minute drive, Alonso practically superglued himself to Joseph's bumper. Catelyn kept a safer distance back probably trying to figure out his motive for agreeing to her presence.

The truth was, Joseph's gut was telling him that Dylan had nothing to do with the disappearance of Kelly or the death of Tracy. What he wasn't completely sure of was whether Dylan had been entirely truthful about his reason for being on the campus. It made sense, and yet...

Hopefully, they would get to the bottom of this and find Kelly before she turned up dead, too.

Catelyn called in her destination and let her captain know Joseph was in town and they'd met up at the crime scene. Dylan was still a suspect, but the evidence thus far was flimsy. He still had his freedom until something else turned up. Whereas Catelyn thought he was guilty, she could tell Joseph believed the boy.

Great.

They were immediately working the case from opposite sides. *God, I know when I became a Christian all those years ago, You never promised me an easy life, but things are getting too complicated too fast. First my mother, now Joseph?*

Catelyn didn't have any doubts about Joseph's investigative skills. That didn't concern her. Working in close proximity with a man she had once had feelings for, did. Of course those feelings were gone now.

Yeah. Right.

No, if she were honest, she'd admit seeing Joseph had un-settled her. In a big way.

She pulled into the driveway of the home that had become her refuge. Thank goodness for Joseph's sister Gina, who'd be-friended Catelyn in high school, or she may never have seen a family as God intended one to be. She'd grown up with the perfect example of what a family *wasn't*. Because of the Santino family, Catelyn grew to love the Lord and came to understand what a personal relationship with Him meant.

Thank you, Lord. Now, about Joseph… She sighed. *I don't even know what to pray, God. Just…be there, please?*

Caught by a long red light, she was the last to arrive. Joseph had parked on the curb, Alonso in the drive off to the side. Joseph, Dylan and Alonso were deep into a signed conversa-tion when Catelyn pulled in behind Joseph. Just as she set the car in Park, a black Jeep swerved around her screeching to a halt, blocking the drive.

She jumped at the sudden intrusion.

What?

A teenager about Alonso's age threw himself from the Jeep and raced toward the boys. The furious expression on his face had Catelyn calling out, "Hey!"

Joseph turned at her yell, concern and shock twisting his features as the boy didn't stop, but tackled Dylan to the ground and began pummeling him with both fists, his shrieks of outrage piercing her ears. Alonso threw himself into the fight, trying to protect his friend.

"Whoa!" Joseph tried to grab a punching fist and caught one on the chin for his effort. His head jerked back and he winced, then waded back in to the fray. This time, he grabbed the boy by his belt and yanked, tossing him to the side. The young guy landed with a grunt, scrambled to his feet and started to lunge back at Dylan. Alonso lurched to take a swing at the teen and Joseph stiff-armed him back.

Catelyn stepped in front of the attacker. The surprise of seeing her had him stumbling to a sudden halt, arms pinwheeling, feet dancing backward.

Adrenaline rushing at the surprise attack, she placed a hand against his chest and shoved, mimicking Joseph's method to keep his brother out of the action. Knocked off balance, the boy went down on his rear. Noticing his hearing aids, she signed to him, "Stop, now."

Joseph had Dylan's arms pinned down, but the boy wasn't struggling, although it looked like he wanted to. Joseph let him go, and Dylan shook his arms then reached up to dab at a cut above his right eye. Alonso hauled himself to his feet. "Chad? What do you think you're doing?" he signed furiously.

"He killed Tracy!"

"He did not!" Alonso protested. "How could you even think that?" Four hands flew through the conversation. Joseph eyed Catelyn with a warning to stay out of it for now. She backed off and watched the boys yell at each other.

Dylan defended himself, saying, "I was there with Kelly, but I left. Tracy was fine when I left. I don't know what happened later."

"You knew Tracy wanted Kelly to break up with you and you told her to stay out of it 'or else.' I saw you."

Dylan looked shocked, then nodded. "Yeah, I did, but I didn't mean I'd kill her. Get real, man. I just meant I wouldn't have anything else to do with her. I'd get her blackballed from the group." He threw his hands up in the air as though in disbelief.

Catelyn almost believed Dylan. He looked so convincing. She fingered the scar on her left arm. Yeah, so had the kid who knifed her in thanks for giving him the benefit of the doubt. She wasn't falling for that one again.

"We need to either go down to the department where we can hash this all out or find a spot around here to get to the bottom of this." She pulled out her notebook and pen.

Joseph motioned to the porch. Chad's hands shook, his fury still palpable, but Catelyn detected grief beneath the anger. Tracy must have meant a lot to him. And what was that about Tracy wanting Kelly to break up with Dylan?

"Joseph, can you give Dylan's and Chad's parents a call and let them know what's going on? I want to do this by the book. I'm not making an arrest—yet—so we can do this here, but I definitely want these parents aware of what's going on. Plus, Chad's in no shape to drive home. Someone needs to get his car."

He pulled his BlackBerry out. "Sure." He got the numbers from a reluctant Chad and a still-fuming Dylan. Soon he had Chad's parents on the way and had left a message for Dylan's mother and one for the kid's father. They were divorced, but shared custody.

"If this turns into an official investigation interrogation, we'll have to move it downtown," Joseph warned.

"Of course. Right now, I just want to talk to Dylan. Informally. He's over fourteen, I don't need his parents' permission for that."

Nodding, Joseph took a seat on the swing. The still-glowering, yet subdued boys sat in opposite corners of the porch. Catelyn planted herself in a rocker between them. She kept silent hoping one of them would be ready to burst forth with information by the time she got around to asking some questions.

The door to the house swung open and Alonso's father, Geovani Santino, stepped out.

"I heard a bunch of commotion out here." Spying Dylan, he signed, "What happened to your eye?"

"My friend went nutso on me." Dylan's fingers flew, hands shaped the words and his glare notched up a bit in intensity. Chad Markham, a student at the deaf school and a member of the high school baseball team, fumed, fists clenched at his side.

Joseph raised a calming hand, then watched as a compact car pulled in behind Chad's Jeep. Chad noticed it, too, and snapped his lips together in a mutinous expression of defiance.

Chad's parents bolted from the car and raced up the porch. "Chad? What's going on?" His mother stopped on the top step taking everything in.

Joseph intervened, introduced everyone and explained the situation. Catelyn let him take over. He looked at her face. Take over for now, anyway.

He made sure the parents knew that this wasn't a formal interrogation. Rather just a "getting together" to see what they could come up with and see if any new information came to light.

Once everyone was settled, Catelyn asked, "Chad, tell us why you think Dylan had something to do with Tracy's death and Kelly's disappearance."

"Because he was there. He said he left, but he didn't, at least I don't believe him. He and Kelly and Tracy all had a huge argument earlier that day. He was really mad at Tracy and told her she'd better watch her mouth, or else. I'm Kelly's friend, her best friend. She was tired of Dylan always telling her who she could hang out with and who she couldn't. She told me so."

Catelyn cocked a brow Dylan. The boy leaned over and grasped his head with his hands. She tapped him on the shoulder and signed, "That true?"

A huge sigh rippled through him. "Yes."

"Anything else you want to add? Because while you keep insisting on your innocence, you're sure leaving out some chunks of need-to-know information."

Dylan shook his head. "We argued. So what? We argued all the time. Tracy didn't like me and didn't try to hide it. I didn't like her, either. She was bossy and pushy and…"

"And what?" Joseph practically growled.

"And Kelly's best friend." He shot a glance at Chad. "Not him. Tracy wanted Kelly to break up with me and date her brother, Zachary. I was afraid…" He trailed off again, rubbing his eyes as though trying to erase a headache. Everyone sat silent. "I was afraid she was going to convince Kelly I wasn't good enough for her so I told her to mind her own business and keep her mouth shut."

"Why didn't you tell us this when we had you in for questioning?" Catelyn demanded.

Tears filled the boy's eyes. "Because it makes it look like I had a reason to…do…something to Tracy." He stood and paced from one end of the porch to the other. Then turned to say, "But I didn't! I swear! I mean, I sure didn't like her, but I would never *hurt* her."

Joseph frowned at the constant protestations of innocence. He watched Catelyn's expressions, her eyes. The more the boy talked, the more she became convinced he did do something. And Joseph had a moment of wondering himself. Could it be that Dylan *had* killed Tracy? Possibly in a fit of anger? An accident?

Blunt-force trauma was the cause of death. Had he picked up a rock and hit her? Pushed her down so she cracked her head against something? But there'd been no sign of that kind of thing at the crime scene. No, the murder weapon was portable.

And the killer either ditched it far enough from the crime scene that the crime-scene unit didn't come across it—or he still had it.

More questioning led nowhere. Dylan said he wouldn't press charges as long as Chad left him alone. The boys were told to stay away from each other, and Chad's parents took him home. Alonso went to his room and shut the door. Dylan's mother, who finally arrived, was filled in on the incident. She expressed her concern, asking to be kept in the loop if anything new happened in the investigation. His father never showed up.

After the mass departure, Catelyn studied the floor of the porch, thinking. She felt in her gut the kid knew way more than he was telling, she just couldn't prove it.

But she would.

Alonso would be upset, and Joseph would hurt for his brother, but…

She stood, straightened her spine as she walked toward her car. He was a cop. A good one. He wouldn't argue the arrest if she had enough evidence, knew he would be right there with her reading the kid his rights if it came down to it. Granted, Dylan's jacket turning up at the scene didn't look good, but his explanation was reasonable. Girls wore their boyfriends' jackets all the time.

So far, nothing had come back from the lab, but she didn't really expect anything this early even with the rush she knew would be on the evidence. With a missing teen, time was of the essence. She'd call Sandy Newman, a tech in the crime lab and a woman Catelyn called friend, to see if Sandy could rush it even faster.

"Hey."

She stopped, turned to find Joseph leaning against a porch pillar, watching her. This time her shiver had nothing to do with anger. She remembered how it felt to slip into his arms and rest her head against his broad shoulder, remembered what it felt like to feel secure, safe. As if the rest of the world didn't matter and everything would be all right.

His sudden change of expectations about certain things in their relationship had crushed her. She'd grown up promising herself she'd be different than her parents, have a different life, a solid marriage.

At first, she'd never thought about dating Joseph simply because he was already rising through the ranks of the local police department.

Then one night, they'd been sitting outside talking after a huge family meal and he'd asked her if she'd like to go on a date with him. She'd hesitated because of his profession, then assured herself that this was Joseph. He knew her dreams, her hopes— her career. During the time she'd been at the academy, all through school, he'd supported her, encouraged her. And so it had begun. She'd fallen head over heels in love with him and he with her.

Until he'd suddenly started talking about "after we're married." About how he was excited because he would make enough money to allow her to stay home. And how God had blessed him in allowing him to find a woman who held the same values as his mother.

And her world had come crashing down. She couldn't believe what she was hearing. He wanted her to shelve her career and become the kind of wife she'd vowed never to be.

At least it had seemed sudden, she thought. Had the signs been there the entire time and she'd just chosen to ignore them?

She'd been devastated that he would ask her to give up *her* career to make *him* happy. No way. She knew where that argument would lead.

And yet she couldn't deny the attraction between them had sizzled, both physically and emotionally. She'd been drawn to his softer side, the one he refused to allow anyone to really see. That, and the fact that, deep down, he had a heart for comforting hurting people.

And it was definitely still there—the attraction, all of it. She held her tongue and just looked at him, hoping her face didn't reveal her inner turmoil.

Finally, he started toward her, hands jammed into his pockets. "Can we talk?"

"About what?"

"Us."

"That's not even a topic, Joseph. There is no 'us,' hasn't been for a while now."

"There could be. What we had, Catie…"

She ignored the shortened version of her name. He only called her that when they were alone.

"*Had*. As in the past. You never once said anything about me quitting my job until I was halfway in love with you and thinking marriage. And then you come out with these expectations and blindsided me."

"I didn't realize…and you shut me out."

"Yes, I did."

"Without even giving us a chance to work through it."

"It wouldn't have mattered. You simply reinforced what I already knew. Why it wouldn't be a good idea to marry a cop." She threw her hands up. "And why are we even having this conversation anyway? Look. Your brother's friend is in trouble. Let's just see where all this ends up before we do anything stupid like talk about…us."

His jaw clenched; his fingers curled into a fist. "If you— we—have to arrest Dylan, I'll have to figure out how to help Alonso deal with it. But for now, we have to work together. Without letting our past interfere. Can we do that?"

"We can try."

"Deal."

He reached out to grasp her hand in a handshake and the tingles that danced up her arm told her she might talk a good game about ignoring their feelings for each other, but actually putting her words into actions was going to take a lot more work than she'd bargained for.

THREE

Joseph stared over Catelyn's shoulder at the autopsy report. Nothing new there. And nothing new about his inability to keep himself from noticing how good she smelled. Just like he remembered. A combination of vanilla shampoo and strong coffee.

"Hey, look at this," she said, just as he inched back a tad to put a little distance between his nose and her hair. She pointed to the list of items found with Tracy. "An iPod. An expensive one."

"Did they run the serial number on it?"

"Yes, and would you look at that?"

"Stolen."

"That kind of makes you sit up and go, 'hmm,' doesn't it?"

"So what does a deaf kid do with an iPod. She must not have been totally deaf. Who reported it stolen?"

She shuffled to the next page. "Here. The Whites. Abe and Eva White on the west side of town."

"A breaking and entering. There's been a rash of those lately, hasn't there?"

"Yep. The guys working it think it's gang related, but haven't been able to connect any specific members to the break-ins yet."

"This might be your connection right here. Go back to the autopsy report."

She did and he pointed out the tattoo. "She had a tattoo of a skull around her belly button."

"The symbol of the new and up-and-coming local gang, The Skulls. We just had a whole session on gang training a month ago."

Joseph sighed. "So now they've infiltrated the deaf school."

"But Tracy spent the majority of her school day at the regular high school. It could be that the gang's not originating on the deaf campus, but the local high school campus."

"Or neither."

"Right. So Tracy was a gang member, we know that much. She's also in possession of stolen merchandise. Which brings me to the questions: Does Dylan know about this? Does he know anything about the breaking and entering and thefts going on? Is he a member of the gang?"

"A lot of good questions." He closed his eyes, picturing Alonso's thin, but well-muscled frame. He shook his head. "I can't remember my brother having a tattoo, but I haven't seen him without his shirt, either. I can't imagine him getting involved in that, but I'll ask Alonso later."

Catelyn shot him a look that said she thought he had his rose-tinted glasses back on. Thankfully, she kept her opinion to herself. He'd have to prove Dylan's innocence one way or another. And if the kid was guilty…

"Did Dylan ever say why Tracy was so adamant about Kelly breaking up with him?"

Joseph shook his head. "Nothing specific. Just that her brother wanted to go out with Kelly and she kept turning him down because she was Dylan's girlfriend."

"What's Tracy's brother's name again?"

"Zachary."

"So, we need to talk to Zachary about this gang that his sister was a part of."

"Looks like. And my bet is that if she was a part of it, so is he."

"He's not deaf. He's hearing and goes to Esterman High." She pushed back from her desk and wisps of blond hair tickled his chin sending shards of longing to clench his gut. Somehow, some way, they were going to have to work things out because she had already burrowed her way under in skin in less than twenty-four hours. Just the thought of telling her goodbye again was painful enough to know that having to go through the real thing again would probably rip his heart to shreds.

Pushing aside his personal agenda, he said, "I suppose we should give the family a call and let them know we want to talk to Zachary. I'm guessing he's probably not back at school yet so soon after Tracy's death."

Catelyn got on the phone and made the call. Joseph got up to stretch a minute and say something to one of the other detectives he'd worked with a few years back.

When she hung up, Catelyn turned to him and frowned. "He's not there."

"So, where is he?"

"His mother didn't know. She said he got a text after lunch and said he was going to meet up with a friend. She hasn't heard from him since."

"When's Tracy's funeral?"

"Tomorrow. Visitation is this afternoon."

"I've got a feeling we need to see if he shows up to the visitation."

"And who he shows up with."

Catelyn scanned the sea of faces heading in to pay respects to the family. Mostly teenagers, teachers, probably some church members. The line to greet the family and offer sympathy extended well down the hall to snake around to the entrance to the funeral home. The front door stood open and Joseph waited off to the side, dressed in a suit and tie.

She nearly stumbled in her uncomfortable medium-height heels. She'd never had a problem walking in them before so she couldn't blame her sudden clumsiness on the shoes.

No, it was Joseph. What was she going to do about him? He exuded strength, authority, and was completely at ease in his six-foot-two-inch frame. At five feet eight she didn't consider herself a short woman, but next to him, she always felt petite, feminine. Something that didn't happen very often around other men. And Joseph was definitely the only man who'd ever made her palms sweat. She rubbed them on her black skirt and tried to paste a serene expression on her face.

His smile greeted her with a warmth that nearly caused the upward tilt of her lips to take a downward turn. So much for serenity.

Have a little backbone, Catelyn. And, Lord, if You'd help me control my wayward emotions here, I'd really appreciate it.

He held the door open and she slipped in, nearly jumping out of her skin when his hand dropped to the small of her back. He's only being a gentleman, she told herself. Relax.

Easier said than done. From the back of the line, they waited, watching.

A few more people trickled in, and the line in front of them moved slowly, but consistently. Catelyn kept her eyes peeled. "See him?"

"No, but he's probably with the family in the receiving room. I can't get a good view yet. A few more inches and I'll be able to see if he's in there."

Catelyn lost her balance and stumbled into the person in front of her. Joseph caught her arm before she could do much damage. The woman turned to see who'd knocked against her and Catelyn felt her face flush. "I'm so sorry. I don't wear heels often and…" She trailed off when the woman laughed and waved a hand as though brushing the incident aside.

"Don't worry about it. Happens to the best of us." A frown pinched her brows. "It's a shame, isn't it?"

"I'm sorry?"

The young woman who looked to be in her early forties stood there holding the hand of a child about six years old. She had a brace on her other hand. "Just a shame. Tracy used to babysit for us on a regular basis."

"Oh, so you knew her well?"

"Absolutely. A great kid. Well, a great kid with a lot of faults, but I liked her. Oh, I'm sorry." She held out a hand that Joseph and Catelyn took turns shaking. "I'm Stacy Dillard. My husband, Alan Dillard, is the baseball coach at Esterman High School." She placed a loving hand on the child's head.

"This is Alan Jr."

"I'm six," the little guy piped in. "My mom hurt her hand."

Catelyn smiled at him and shook his hand. "Nice to meet you Alan Jr."

Stacy gave a self-conscious laugh and held up her hand. "Carpal tunnel. Anyway, I wasn't sure if I should bring him or not, but my mother couldn't babysit today and I didn't want to miss…" Tears welled in her eyes and she blinked them back. Taking a deep breath, she blew it out. "Tracy's brother, Zachary, is our catcher."

Joseph spoke up. "Then you know Dylan Carlisle."

The woman's green eyes brightened, the tears fading. "Oh, sure, he used to hang around Zachary quite a lot. We have the team over for cookouts and such about once a month." Her brows drew together in a slight frown. "I haven't seen much of Dylan lately, though. How's he doing? Is he here?"

"He's upset about Tracy, of course, but other than that, he seems to be doing all right. And no, he's not here."

"I know you consider him a suspect, don't you?" When neither Catelyn nor Joseph responded, she frowned. "Alan said you did. Dylan told him about being questioned by the police." She let out a sigh. "I can't see Dylan as having anything to do with Tracy's death. If the police need a suspect, they need to be looking at Zachary, if you ask me." She herded the child in front of her toward the door. "Well, I was waiting for Alan. He told me he'd meet me in the line, but he's probably talking to someone and got held up. I guess I'd better see if I can find him. It's good to meet you."

She started to hurry off, but stopped when Catelyn laid a restraining hand on her arm. "Wait a minute. Why do you say that? About Zachary, I mean."

The woman shrugged. "He and Tracy fought constantly. I even saw him shove her into the fence one day after a game. I don't know what she said to him, but he didn't like it. Tracy and Dylan argued some, too, but Dylan never put his hands on her like Zachary did. I don't have anything other than just my feelings when I say Zachary should be a suspect." She sighed. "And I probably shouldn't have even said anything. Excuse me." This time Catelyn didn't stop her as she hurried off.

Catelyn looked at Joseph. "So Zachary plays on the baseball team and has a temper. And Dylan is known to hang out with him. Teammates and friends?"

"No crime in that. She also said she hadn't seen Dylan in a while." He thought for a moment. "Maybe the boys are former friends. I'll have to ask Alonso and see what he says. Maybe it's as simple as Dylan and Zachary had a falling out and he was avoiding being around him. That would explain why she hadn't seen Dylan around—because he was doing his best to stay out of trouble."

"Maybe."

"I still want to know if Zachary's a part of this gang. And who he was with earlier while his family was at home grieving."

"As soon as we can get to him, we'll find out."

She spotted Stacy Dillard coming back her way. The poor thing looked harried. "I guess I'll just wait here. I can't find Alan anywhere." Still clutching Alan Jr.'s hand, she slipped back into the line in front of Catelyn and Joseph. "Do you mind if I take my spot back?"

"Of course not. Go ahead."

Stacy did and started talking to the person in front of her.

Catelyn stepped to the side to peer around the shifting line of bodies and into the visitation room. "I think I see him," she told Joseph. "Standing next to his mother and younger brother."

"Yep, that's him."

"Just a little closer. Oh, look, everyone's standing."

Zachary shook the next person's hand, looking uncomfortable in his black suit and red tie. Tall, with the build of a natural athlete, he shifted, his eyes moving to and fro. He didn't even bother to try and smile to the people offering condolences; in fact, he looked ready to bolt.

Catelyn leaned in a little closer to Joseph. "You got your running shoes on?"

"I was just thinking the same thing. Why would he run, though? We just want to talk to him?"

"Maybe he thinks that *we* think he knows something."

"Yeah, and he's scared he'll tell us if we catch him."

"Then let's catch him."

Two more steps forward. Zachary's eyes raised, caught on Catelyn's, flitted to the man beside her and widened. The fear in his face couldn't be missed, not even with the distance still between them.

Sweat turned his face shiny and he shifted, glanced at his

mother's back, his sister in the now-closed coffin—and the door on the other side of the room.

"He's gonna make a run for it," Joseph predicted.

"I'm going to cover the other door. You get him from this side."

"Right."

Catelyn slipped out of line and headed down the short hall to the door that opened to the hallway around the corner. The open balcony above her now stood empty, occupied only moments before by friends and family who were now greeting the bereaved. If Zachary made it outside to his car, she'd lose him. Or he would have plenty of hiding places in the cemetery with the huge markers.

Rounding the corner, she was just in time to see a figure dart from the visitation room and head in the opposite direction.

"Zachary, stop! We just want to talk!"

The teen looked back once and kept going, picking up the pace to a fast jog.

Joseph came out of the room. He must have cut through in pursuit. No one else followed, so it must have been done discreetly.

"That way," she pointed.

Together, they took off after the teen, then heard a door slam.

At the sound of a loud crack, Catelyn stopped, turned shocked eyes to Joseph who looked back at her with the same expression she knew her face wore.

"Gunshot?"

Catelyn pulled her weapon, shouting into her radio, "Shots fired," as she raced to the door, yelling at everyone to get down. Joseph was two steps behind her, his gun drawn and ready. Shoving it open, she pulled to a stop, the sight before her sending horror up her spine.

Zachary lay in the middle of the parking lot, unmoving, blood pooling under his head.

FOUR

Five minutes later, the ambulance screamed into the parking lot across the street. In spite of the seriousness of the situation, they'd wait for the all-clear from the officers before they'd approach the scene. No matter who was hurt or how bad it was, for their own safety, medical personal could not enter the scene until it was deemed safe by officers.

Was the boy dead? Where were his parents? Were they still shaking hands with visitors, unaware their oldest son possibly lay dying—or was already dead?

Joseph gripped the tie he'd yanked from his neck, wishing he had the shooter by the throat instead. After the gunshot, Catelyn had secured the area, then bolted toward the fallen boy, placing her own life in danger, doing what she could for him while keeping an eye on the area around her.

Joseph had raced to the balcony after the shooter, knowing he was probably too late.

He found nothing but a spent cartridge. The shooter had disappeared as quickly as he'd appeared. Joseph radioed to let EMS know they could approach.

He looked around again. The person had left in a hurry and hadn't bothered to clean up. Joseph turned back inside, studying the room. The shooter had either come up the stairs or the elevator. Joseph would bet the stairs in case there was a camera in the elevator.

But they'd check it anyway.

He walked over to a door just off the room. Twisted the knob. Locked. The sign said Employees Only.

"Excuse me, sir?"

Joseph turned to see a dark-suited man with a name tag that read Butler Dietz. Joseph asked, "What are you doing up here? Can you open this room?"

The man's brow furrowed. "I work here." He pulled a set of keys from his pocket, located the right one and unlocked the door. Joseph glanced in.

A room full of coffins. And everything looked relatively undisturbed. He spoke into his radio, "Set up a perimeter, question everyone, don't let anyone leave the scene." An affirmative answer squawked back at him.

He turned the worker, saying, "Okay, thanks. I need you out of here, too. This is a crime-scene and I need to keep it preserved."

Flustered, the man nodded and headed for the stairs, meeting a swarm of cops coming up. Joseph motioned for one of the officers to escort the man down, then filled the rest of them in on the situation. "Crime-scene unit's on the way."

"We've got this covered," a tall officer assured Joseph.

Joseph loped back down the steps to find Catelyn watching a man work on Zachary, the EMTs offering their assistance as it was requested.

She looked up at his approach, question in her eyes.

Joseph pursed his lips and shook his head. "No, he got away."

"He?"

A shrug. "He, she. Whoever. The shooter's gone. Crime scene unit's on the way. Uniforms are preserving the scene." He pointed to the man on his knees beside Zachary. "Who's this guy?"

"A doctor. He insisted on trying to help."

The man looked up. "I was late coming from the hospital for the funeral. I'm a friend of the Merritts. When I saw all the commotion, I thought I'd see if I could help." He looked back down at Zachary who lay still and pale. "The bullet grazed his head. It didn't enter the skull, which is a good thing, but it might have fractured it. I've called a neurologist. He'll be waiting at the hospital when we get there."

"Thanks."

A man rushed up and said, "Oh my…can I do anything?"

"Who are you?" Joseph queried.

"I'm Alan Dillard, the baseball coach at Esterman High. Zachary was…is one of my players. What's going on? Who would do such a…"

"Zachary! Oh, no, oh, my…" Joseph turned to see Zachary's mother rushing from the mortuary. The boy's father was right behind with the younger brother bringing up the rear.

"What happened? What's going on? Why is this happening?" The distraught woman wailed her grief, echoing the coach's questions. Two of her three children: one dead and one severely wounded. His heart went out to her.

Alan Dillard grabbed the woman's shoulder, keeping her from throwing herself across her son and impeding the work being done on him. "He's getting the help he needs, ma'am."

The EMTs let the doctor take the lead, securing Zachary's neck in a brace, then they gently loaded the boy onto the gurney. The doctor helped, supervising the transfer, then washing his hands with the special alcohol-based soap the EMTs left for him. The ambulance pulled out, siren wailing, on the way to the hospital.

Joseph clapped the man on the shoulder. "Thanks. He might have a chance because you were here."

"Quinn Carson." The doctor introduced himself, holding out a hand for Joseph to shake.

"Joseph Santino. That's my partner, Catelyn Clark."

Catelyn nodded and gave a half smile. The ambulance disappeared around a curve.

"I need to get to the hospital. I need to be with my boy." Zachary and Tracy's mother wailed.

Dr. Carson turned to take the woman in his arms. "Sarah, I'm so sorry. Go and I'll be there to check on him shortly."

"Come on, Mrs. Merritt, Mr. Merritt. I'll do anything I can to help. I'll stay here and make sure everything's finished up. Go be with Zachary," Alan offered, his face creased in sympathy and concern.

Tears flowing, cheeks ashen, the woman nodded and took her friend's advice. She, her husband and young son hurried to their car and took off for the hospital. Friends and family dispersed to their own vehicles in near silence, shock rendering them speechless.

Friday morning, Catelyn dragged into work feeling the weight of the world on her shoulders. After Tracy's murder, she'd talked to her parents extensively, but they'd been basically clueless about their daughter's activities. She sighed.

Unfortunately, parents had to work and couldn't watch their teens twenty-four/seven, but still, she would've thought they would have been able to provide more information than they had.

First thing this morning, she'd called to check on Zachary and learned he still hadn't awakened. She did learn that his abdomen sported the same tattoo his sister had. They posted a guard on his door who would also call immediately if Zachary woke up.

A quick call to a buddy who worked in the gang unit confirmed that Zachary was definitely part of the gang and had a record for some petty theft, shoplifting and one incident involving a stolen car. Although, it seemed that since baseball season had started, he'd kept his nose clean.

Deep in thought, Catelyn set her cup of coffee on her desk and tossed her purse in the bottom drawer.

"Good morning to you, too."

She whirled to find Joseph cranked back in an old squeaky chair someone had scavenged from the storage room. A desk had been set up and he looked quite at home. Lovely.

"Hi, didn't see you there. Looks like you're all set up." She hoped her aggravation wasn't too obvious.

"Bugs you, huh?"

Clamping her teeth on her lower lip to control her tongue, she took a deep breath. It was all about self-control. Before allowing herself to respond, she picked up three phone messages and read them.

Set them back down.

Picked up her coffee and took a swig.

Then she turned to face him. And ignored his taunt. "What time did you get here?"

"About an hour ago."

Was he trying to show her up? He'd soon learn she didn't play that game. No, she'd grown up watching her parents trying to outdo each other, show the other who was the better cop. Catelyn had decided she'd avoid that immature behavior.

Actually, if she was honest, she didn't remember that particular trait about Joseph. Was she just being…defensive? She did remember that could be a big tease, so maybe…he was teasing her?

Withholding judgment, she kept her cool.

He said, "I couldn't sleep so figured I'd just come on in." No sarcasm, no in-your-face attitude. Just fact.

That was a trait she was more comfortable with.

Relaxing, she settled in her chair. "I guess we need to plan out our day."

"I've got some ideas. Do you mind if I run them by you?"

Asking her permission? This she didn't remember. Suspicious, she eyed him. Then offered a shrug. "Sure. Fire away."

A warm smile creased his cheeks and crinkled his eyes. Familiar attraction zinged, and Catelyn deliberately stomped on it.

"First of all, I want to get a record of Zachary's text messages. Then, I thought we might make our way over to the crime lab and see if we can light a fire under someone. I want those DNA results back."

"I checked on Zachary this morning and he's still unconscious. He's got some pretty serious neurological stuff going on. Swelling on his brain and fluid. They've even put him on a ventilator." She shook her head. "They're not sure if he'll ever wake up. The principal of the school and Coach Dillard are letting the students organize a fund-raiser for medical expenses for Zachary. The deaf school offered its services, too. Apparently, Alan is well liked in the deaf community, thanks to his having deaf parents."

Joseph nodded. "That's a great thing to do and it'll give the students something constructive to focus on. They've got to be traumatized by all that's happened over the last few days."

"To say the least. The school counselors are working overtime right now, talking in the classrooms, counseling friends of Tracy, Kelly and Zachary. They're doing all they can do. They've even called in some outside help, so that's good."

"I'm glad to hear that. I just hope someone is helping the Merritt family. To have something so awful happen to two of your children…it's beyond my imagination."

Sympathy clouded her gaze for a brief moment. She nodded

and said, "I want to know what it is those two kids knew that someone was willing to commit murder in order to keep it secret."

"And I want to talk to Kelly Franklin's brother today, too. His name is Billy. Let's see if he can shed some light on his sister's disappearance."

"Sound like we've got our game plan."

"Oh, and Alonso's got a baseball game tonight. I'm planning on catching it if you want to join me."

Speechless for a moment, Catelyn processed his statement. Gathering her wits, she shrugged. "We'll see."

He raised an eyebrow, but didn't comment on her evasiveness.

As they headed out, Catelyn ignored the excitement building within her at the thought of spending so much time in Joseph's company. Excitement or no, she reminded herself that this was the man who'd broken her heart two years ago and there was no way she was trusting him with the pieces ever again.

Pulling into the parking lot of the building that housed the local crime lab, Joseph pondered the situation silently while Catelyn called Billy Franklin's mother to ask for permission to visit him at the school, assuring the woman that Billy was in no way considered a suspect, but they just wanted to see if he had anything else to add that might help them find his sister. Sometimes people remembered things later. After the dust settled, and the adrenaline wore off.

Tracy had been killed, and Kelly had disappeared. Why?

What did Tracy know that was worth killing for? Had Kelly been at the scene? Had she witnessed the murder and fled? Was she hiding out? Or had she witnessed it and been taken against her will? And why hadn't the killer just killed her, too? Or had he and they just hadn't found her body yet?

Sighing, Joseph waited until Catelyn hung up from a second

call before swinging his long frame from the car. "Who was that? It sounded official."

"Victor."

"What did he want?"

"An arrest."

"Don't we all? I vote for arresting the right person, though."

"I know." She pulled at her lower lip with her two top teeth as she thought. Joseph cut his eyes and swallowed hard. He clearly remembered kissing those lips and wanted to do it again. He blinked and focused back in on what she was saying. "I still think Dylan's up to his eyeballs in this thing and knows a lot more than he's telling."

"Possibly. It's just that when he protested his innocence so profusely, I believed him. I didn't see anything that made me think he was covering up a murder."

Catelyn rolled her eyes at him. "Trust me. Kids like that learn how to lie so convincingly *they* probably even believe what they're saying. But they're liars all the same."

"Kids like that?" Joseph raised a brow. Why was she so cynical? He didn't remember seeing this side of her before. Wary about a romantic relationship? Yes. A tough street cop? Yes. But where had her compassion gone? What had happened to change that part of her?

She must have read something in his face because she asked, "I sound harsh, don't I?"

"Yeah, you do."

She chewed her lip again. Then pulled her jacket off and rolled up her sleeve. He sucked in a deep breath. A thin five-inch jagged scar made its way from the inside of her elbow to the center of her arm just falling short of her wrist.

He reached out and pulled it toward him for a closer look. Angry, puckered and red, yet healing. "Compliments of one of *those* kids?"

"Yeah."

"So, you learned your lesson, is that what you're saying? And every kid is guilty until proven innocent?"

She flushed and yanked out of his light grasp. "Something like that."

He let her go. "When did that happen?"

"About six months ago."

He winced. "Ouch."

Shutters came down over her eyes. "Yep."

"You want to tell me about it?" She used to tell him everything. His heart hurt at the memories. He'd missed her. Her laugh, her beauty, her spunk, the way she made him feel when she let him see the pride she felt for him when he collared a criminal. The way she melted into his arms for a snuggle on the couch. Her kisses...

"Nothing much to tell. I had the kid cornered, he acted like he wasn't going to give me any trouble, just blubbering about how he'd been set up. I believed him, let my guard down and he pulled a knife from somewhere. And before you ask, yes, I'd already patted him down. I made a stupid mistake and missed it. It was a little thing, but it hurt. So, no more trusting crying teens protesting their innocence." Subject closed. "Let's go see what we can find out about the DNA. I hope this isn't a wasted trip."

He smiled and let it drop even though he wanted to pursue the fact that just because she had one bad experience with one kid didn't mean they were all the same. But he knew when she got that look on her face, attempting to push the subject more wouldn't get him anywhere. So he said, "The personal touch is never wasted. A phone call might have sufficed, but when you're face-to-face, it's harder for them to put you off...or hang up on you."

She gave a rare grin, one he remembered, but hadn't seen since he'd been back. "Very true."

* * *

Why had she bothered to explain about that scar? Catelyn decided having Joseph around could be addictive. Somehow, she was going to have to figure out how to keep her mouth shut around him. Spilling her guts about everything that bothered her was no longer an option. She'd moved on, and he'd just plain *moved*…

"Sandy, how are you?" Catelyn spotted the criminalist and waved her down. A pretty, petite woman in her late thirties, she was part of a team that did their job well. She'd also been one of the people covering Tracy's murder.

The woman's brows arched under her shaggy bangs. "Catelyn? What are you doing here?"

"Trying to solve a murder and find a missing girl. This is my partner, Joseph Santino. He's working on the case with me." Joseph and Sandy shook hands, then Catelyn said, "We need to know if anything's come back on the blood found on the ring."

"Hmm. I'm not sure. We had that murder-suicide on the other side of town and things have been a little crazier than usual around here."

Great. "I hate to be pushy, but do you mind putting a rush on it? There's a killer out there and a missing girl."

Concern flickered across the woman's face. "I heard. I know Greg was working with the ring. Come on and let's see if he's in the lab."

The three marched down the hall and Catelyn couldn't help feeling the thrill, the excitement that came with her job. Sure, she hated the deaths, the psychos out there who caused such pain and misery to others, but she knew she was right where she was supposed to be.

She was born to be a cop. A detective. Her mission in life was to put the bad guys away. She didn't have time for romance or a family—or Joseph.

Right, God? God had been strangely quiet with the answer to that question lately and she wondered if the pang she felt in the vicinity of her heart meant she wasn't exactly on the right track. *Lord?*

She looked at Joseph, his rugged profile so familiar; one she'd never tired of looking at during the time they'd dated. Pain seared her. The loss of his presence in her life left a gaping hole she realized she'd never completely filled.

It was too bad he'd never understood that part of her personality, the cop part; it grieved her that he couldn't accept she'd never be the traditional happy homemaker he envisioned when he pictured his wife.

Unfortunately, she knew this all too well. After all, it's what had broken them up two years ago. Joseph Santino had wanted her to stop being a cop, stay home and be his wife. A mother to his children. Part of her regretted that it wasn't enough; she grieved the loss of his companionship, her best friend.

But there was no way she'd ever give up her career. Not even for the man she loved.

Just wasn't going to happen.

Joseph watched Catelyn in action. She loved her job, that was obvious. He saw her disappointment when Sandy returned with no news. "But I promise to let you know as soon as it's processed. I've got your cell number, and I'll call you myself."

Catelyn agreed and then she and Joseph were headed back out. He asked, "Where to now? Billy Franklin?"

"Yes. Esterman High School."

He climbed behind the wheel again without asking. He knew she preferred to ride rather drive. He was falling comfortably into old routines.

As they drove through the streets, Catelyn looked out the

window. He decided to touch on the past a little. "How's your mom?"

If he'd zapped her with a Taser, he wouldn't have gotten more response. Her head whipped around and she seared him with her gaze. "What?"

"Your mother. How is she?"

"In a nursing home. Dying."

Oops. He hadn't expected that one. He should have done his homework before venturing into uncharted territory. "Aw, Catie, I'm sorry."

She looked back out the window. "You didn't know. Did you let the school know we were coming?"

Her way of saying "Back off." Another topic not up for discussion. But he remembered her mother and genuinely wanted to know about her. Give it time, he told himself.

"Yes, I did." He let the subject drop.

He turned into the parking lot of the high school and she gave him a half grin. "At least you haven't lost your sense of direction."

For a moment he blanked, then the memory rushed forward. The day they'd gone hiking in the North Carolina woods, searching for a specific waterfall.

"This way," he'd insisted, pointing toward a path that branched to the left.

"No Joseph, it's this way. I have it right…"

"Catie, I know exactly where I'm going. Now be quiet so I can concentrate."

They'd wandered around for the next two hours in silence. Finally, he'd stopped and told her he was going to have to call and get directions.

She'd silently handed him her BlackBerry and suggested he follow the map she'd found online two hours ago.

At his stunned expression, she'd laughed herself silly. Humiliated, he'd sat beside her, fuming. But then her infectious giggles eventually got to him, the ability to laugh at himself making its way to the surface, and he'd found himself chuckling along with her.

They'd found the waterfall in a matter of minutes and shared the sweetest kiss he'd ever experienced.

Now, he spotted the glint in her eye. So, she still thought about their times together, too. Interesting. Heartening. Hope rose within him, but instead of making a big deal about it, he gave her a mock glare and said, "Cute."

She laughed and exited the car, leading the way to the front door of the school.

Their mood turned serious as they entered the building. Joseph watched her shutters come back down. All cop now, she was back to business. Flashing her badge at the receptionist, she said, "Did Billy Franklin's mother call to let you know we were coming?"

"Yes, she did."

"Is there a room where we could speak with him privately?"

"Of course."

They walked down a short hall to a conference room. She said, "I'll just page Billy for you."

She left, and Joseph paced.

A few minutes later, the door opened once again and a young man who Joseph knew to be seventeen years old, entered. He had on baggy jeans and a light sweatshirt with the school logo emblazoned across his chest. He looked scared and tired, like he hadn't had much sleep lately.

Probably hadn't. Not with his kid sister missing.

Following Billy was Coach Dillard. "I'm sorry," Joseph stopped his advancement into the room, "You can't be here."

"Billy asked me to join him. Is it all right?"

Joseph looked at Billy then over at Catelyn. She shrugged. "If he wants him here, I guess."

Alan sat next to Billy at the table. "I assume this is about Kelly."

"You assume right," Catelyn said.

Joseph turned his attention back to the boy. "Do you know if Kelly and Tracy were together at the school Tuesday night?"

Billy licked his lips, his eyes darting around the room stopping when he came to Catelyn. "She already questioned me the day Tracy died. Why do I have to answer more?"

"Because Kelly's still missing, Billy, and we're running out of options to help find her. So, if some of our questions seem repetitive, will you just humor us?" Catelyn frowned at Billy's evasiveness. Joseph didn't blame her. He eyed the kid and started to speak when the door opened.

Another man in his early sixties stepped through the door. "I'm Carlton Bowles, principal here. Do you mind if I sit in on this?"

He held out a hand and Joseph and Catelyn stood once again. Joseph said, "Have a seat."

Catelyn decided it was time for a woman's touch. "Billy, I know we talked right after Tracy was found and I appreciate your cooperation. The only reason Special Agent Santino and I are here is because we're hoping you might have remembered something since I last talked to you. You're not a suspect in any way right now. Do you think you could relax and just try to help us out?"

At her reassurance, his countenance seemed to soften. "Yes. Like I said before, I think she and Tracy were together, but I can't say for sure. She texted me a little after 4:00 that afternoon and said she was meeting some friends." He shrugged. "I don't know if that included Tracy or not. She wanted me to make up an excuse to tell Mom and Dad about why she was going to be late for supper. I did."

"And she never came home, right?"

"Right. I wasn't too worried because she was always late, but then she wasn't home by dark, which still wasn't that unusual. Then around 9:00, I mean, she *still* wasn't home…"

She waited to see if he was going to pick back up with his sentence. He didn't, so she said, "I do have one question that I haven't asked you. Do you know anything about the gang, The Skulls?"

Catelyn knew she'd hit a bull's-eye when Billy's face lost all color. His throat bobbed and shook his head. "No, no. I don't know anything about them. Just what I've heard and it's not good. I don't want to be mixed up in that stuff. Uh-uh."

He placed his hands on the table. They trembled and he shoved them back in his lap. This boy was terrified of something.

Alan lifted a hand. "Um, do you mind if I intervene here?"

Catelyn lifted a brow. "Sure."

"Billy's a good kid trying to stay out of trouble. A fantastic baseball player with a huge future ahead of him. That sister of his…well, no disrespect, but she seemed to be heading toward trouble. I mean, I've heard she was a good kid, so maybe I'm off base, but considering the kids she hung out with…" He shrugged. "From the outside looking in, I would say that if she had her way, she would have had Billy involved in that gang."

"Do you know for sure that Kelly was involved?"

"No, like I said, I only have my suspicions. I do know she was good friends with Tracy, the only other girl from the deaf school who was also part of our mainstream program here. You know, where we bus deaf kids over so they can be around their hearing peers. And I know Tracy was involved in the gang. She made no secret of that fact. We also have a few hearing students who claim they're involved in the gang, but as long as they don't cause trouble here at school, there's not much we can do about it."

"Billy?" Catelyn turned to him. "Was Kelly involved with The Skulls?"

The teen buried his face in his hands for a brief moment before looking back up. "No way!" Then he looked at the two men and muttered, "I don't know. But no, I don't think so, although she never said anything to me about it. And I really don't think she would be involved in that anymore than I would. She wasn't like that even though she was friends with Tracy. Kelly did say something about talking to Tracy about the gang, but I think she was going to try and convince her to quit the gang, not ask to join." He shot a look at his coach, refuting the man's earlier comment. To give the man credit, he just shrugged.

Billy went on, "Tracy and Kelly have been friends since they both started preschool at the deaf school, so if Tracy was involved with The Skulls in any way, and I'm pretty sure she was, she probably did ask Kelly to join, but Kelly would never…" He shrugged and looked away again.

Catelyn glanced at Joseph trying to see what he thought. An impassive rock stared back her, but she knew he wasn't missing a thing.

She turned back to Billy. Was this kid telling everything he knew? She couldn't tell. He still looked scared. And that made her suspicious that he knew something else.

She leaned forward. "Look Billy, if Kelly's in trouble, withholding information isn't going to help matters. We're going to get to the bottom of this one way or another."

He threw his hands up. "I don't know anything else. I'm sorry, but…I mean I can make something up if you want, but I don't know what else to tell you."

Alan placed a hand on the teen's shoulder. "Calm down, Billy. They're just trying to do their jobs."

"No, of course I don't want you to make something up,"

Catelyn assured him. "We just don't have much to go on and are doing everything we can to find out what happened to your sister and Tracy. One last question."

"What?"

"Do you think Dylan would hurt Tracy? Did he have any reason to kill her?"

Billy winced then mumbled, "I don't know. I didn't really hang around with Dylan that much even though he was dating Kelly. As for him hurting Tracy, I wouldn't think so, but they had a fight the other day. Kelly told me about it. Zachary, Tracy's brother, wanted Kelly to be his girl."

"And Kelly didn't want that."

"No way. She was all into Dylan."

"All right." Catelyn pressed her palms to the table and stood. "If you think of anything else, you'll call, right?"

"Sure." He licked his lips. "I will. Can I go now?"

"Yeah, go on."

Joseph looked at him. "You have a game tonight, right?"

"Yes, sir."

"Good luck, then. I look forward to watching you play."

Confusion flickered briefly, then he shrugged and said, "Oh, right. You're Alonso's brother. He's told me a lot about you and I've seen your picture. Thanks."

The boy and his coach left. The principal stood and shoved his hands in his pockets. "We want to do everything we can to help Billy. I don't think he would have anything to do with Tracy's death or Kelly's disappearance. He's our star baseball player. Our pitcher. He spends his time on the field. He doesn't hang out with the wrong kind of kids."

"Star pitcher, huh? Scholarship material?"

Pride puffed out Carlton's chest. "National Baseball League material for high school kids, then on to the majors. He's going to put this school on the map. You just wait and see. A couple of years ago, the district was going to cut the team, the whole program, due to a lack of funds. Thanks to an anonymous donor, we got the money. We already had the best coach in the country. Put those two together…" He rubbed his hands together in what Joseph would call glee. "Now, Billy and Coach Dillard are the ones taking the team all the way this year. It's going to be big. So, whatever I can do to help you with this case to make sure Billy stays in the clear, you just let me know."

Joseph frowned. "We're not investigating this to keep Billy in the clear. If Billy's guilty of something, Billy'll take the fall for it."

"I know, I just meant…"

Catelyn jumped in, saying, "Coach Dillard seems very involved with his students."

"Definitely." The man looked relieved at Catelyn's intervention. "All of our coaches are. He even takes a couple of them to church every week. Just the ones who want to go and don't have a ride. We certainly don't force anything on anyone. Alan's also an avid hunter and takes a group up into North Carolina every year. He says it teaches his students patience."

"Sounds like the school is lucky to have him," Joseph said.

"Definitely." They shook hands again.

The secretary popped her head in. "You're needed in the cafeteria, sir."

"Thanks, Alice." He turned back. "Can you two see yourselves out?"

"Absolutely. Thanks again for your cooperation."

"Anytime."

He left and Joseph looked at Catelyn. "Billy knows something, and he'd scared stiff to tell us what it is."

"I got that feeling, too."

"What do you think about the coach?"

Shrugging, she moved toward the door. "He seems nice enough, I guess. Supports his students, a concerned teacher."

"He's also in the running for the Amateur Baseball Association's coach of the year. His team is going to the High School Baseball World Series in July and he's got colleges and the National Baseball League looking at him. Like Mr. Bowles said, Billy's his star pitcher. Colleges all over are looking to snatch him up as soon as he graduates. And the man doesn't want anything to happen to shake that up. I think he'd protect Billy with his life if it came down to it." Joseph shook his head. "And although he comes across concerned and solicitous, I bet he wouldn't feel the same way if it was just his average student in trouble."

"Possibly. Then again, you never know. And how do you know all that about him anyway?"

He grinned. "I read the newspaper."

"Huh. Sounds like Coach has a lot going on."

Catelyn's phone rang, cutting her off. "Hello?"

"Hey, it's Sandy, in the crime lab."

"Sandy." Anticipation jumpstarted her heart rate. "What did you find?"

"The DNA came back with a match for the blood on the ring. You'll *never* guess who."

Catelyn took the information and looked at Joseph smugly as she hung up.

FIVE

"The DNA matched up with Dylan's. I'm shocked."

"Do I detect a tad of sarcasm in that statement?"

They rushed to the car, Catelyn heading for the passenger seat. "Maybe a tad."

"So it was Dylan's?"

"Yup."

Joseph heaved a sigh and climbed in. "I suppose you want to arrest him?"

Looking him in the eye, she said, "No, I don't *want* to, I have to. I'm sorry for Alonso, but I'm not surprised at this development. Dylan claimed he was never there. And now his DNA shows up on her ring?"

"Could have happened before that night."

"The blood was fresh. She hadn't been there long before the security guard found her."

Joseph fell silent for a couple of minutes. "The cut on his chin," he said, almost to himself.

"What?"

"The day he came to the crime scene at the school. I was thinking how Alonso and his buddies were growing up, then realized they were past growing, they were pretty much grown. Dylan had a cut on his chin and I thought he'd probably gotten it shaving. If that's Dylan's DNA on the ring, then Tracy must have slapped him, hit him or something…maybe backhanded him, depending on which way her ring was turned."

"Let's go pick him up. He's at the deaf school. He's a part of the mainstream program even though he does most of his classes here at the high school. Alonso loves the program because he has the opportunity to be around his hearing friends and be at the deaf school, too."

She got on the phone with the deaf school and confirmed Dylan was on campus and informed them they were on the way with a warrant for his arrest. An officer would meet them there with the warrant. The school would call Dylan's mother and let her know what was going on. Joseph drove through town going slower than she would have liked. "You still don't think he's guilty, do you?"

"No, I don't. I think evidence can be misleading. I like to have all the facts before making a decision."

Was he implying that she didn't? Catelyn thought they had more than enough facts. "What about his jacket being at the scene? The ring with his DNA? The fact that he obviously lied about being there?"

"I agree. No doubt, evidence is there, but is it the right evidence or simply circumstantial? Sorry, I just…it's a gut thing."

She couldn't discount that. Not when her gut had saved her life more than once. Instead, she turned her thoughts toward arresting the kid, telling herself she was doing the right thing. Doing what she had to do.

Like her job.

No matter what anyone else said or argued. She was a good cop. She'd do a good job. Period.

If the kid was innocent, his lawyer would prove it.

Joseph got into contact with the school resource officer and put the man on notice that they were on the way to arrest one of his students.

They arrived at the school and Joseph noticed the activity on the campus. Hands gestured, fingers flew in conversation. Students walking to and from class. A lot of laughter going on. Unfortunately, one student wasn't going to be laughing when he was arrested.

The deaf school principal knew they were coming and stood outside the building to greet them. In his early thirties, he stood around six feet tall, had a dash of gray at his temples and a commanding presence. He welcomed them with a pained smile and a handshake. "I'm Cole Pierson. Are you sure you've got the right person?"

Catelyn sighed. "The evidence says we do."

Shaking his head, he led the way back inside, saying, "I'm having a hard time with this one. I know I've only been here a short time, a couple of months since the last principal retired, but I've gotten to know these kids pretty well. Dylan comes from a tough background, but I can't see him doing this. Especially not to poor Tracy. He worshipped that girl."

Catelyn cocked a brow. "In certain circumstances, worship can turn to hatred real quick."

"That's true, I suppose. I just…" Cole shook his head again. "Well, let's get to it. We didn't put the school on lockdown, but our school resource officer has gone to get him. He'll bring him to the conference room."

As they headed in that direction, a young woman came hurrying down the hall, speaking and signing at the same time, "Dylan's gone. Kevin came by to get him, but he wasn't in my classroom. I think he figured something out and has run."

Catelyn demanded, "Which way did he go?"

"He came in my classroom for a brief minute, then left. When he went out, he turned left, so he either went to the restroom…or out the end door."

Joseph ran for the exit, Catelyn bolted for the one on the opposite end of the hall, thinking they could close in on him and catch in the middle.

Twenty minutes later, they gave up the search on the campus.

"If he's still on school grounds, we'll never find him," Joseph declared with disgust. "We'd have to get the K-9 unit out here to track him down."

"Yeah, I bet he knows this place like the back of his hand, including all nooks and crannies to hide in." Catelyn stood for a moment, thinking. "And if he's not on campus…where would you go if you were a scared deaf kid?"

Joseph watched her, seeing the wheels clicking in her mind. He answered, "Someplace I'd feel safe, to someone I could count on to help me out and not turn me in."

They looked at each other and said, simultaneously, "Alonso."

Realizing it was probably a waste of time, but having to check in spite of his gut feeling, Joseph raced back into the school building asked the secretary to call Alonso to the office. In the meantime, Joseph tried to text message his brother, however, he got no response even after several attempts. But then, Joseph reasoned, if Alonso was in class, he wouldn't have his phone on.

And if he was trying to help Dylan, he wouldn't bother answering Joseph's text messages. Joseph had a feeling it was the latter.

The secretary looked up from the black notebook. "He didn't sign out, but I called the security guard who said he drove off campus about ten minutes ago."

Joseph hit the glass door at a run and slammed himself into the car. Catelyn gave him a questioning look and Joseph answered it, "He left campus."

"This isn't good."

Grimly, he told, "I'm aware of that. Let's catch up to them before anyone else spots them." Thinking fast, he told her, "Seems to me, every deaf kid I know has a phone simply for text messaging purposes, a Sidekick, a BlackBerry, whatever. Can we track his phone?"

"Do you have his number?"

"No." Joseph shook his head, then smiled and said, "No, but I've got Alonso's. If we're right and they're together, we can find them that way."

Pulling out her cell, she said, "Give me the number."

He did and she put the request in to the person on the other end. "Call me when you've got it. Thanks." Hanging up she looked at him. "I also put out a Be on the Lookout, a BOLO, for Dylan's car and Alonso's. Both cars are missing from the student lot. If they're in either one, they won't get far. The security guard said both boys left at approximately the same time. I have a feeling Dylan's going to ditch his car and hook up with Alonso."

Joseph said, "I would say that's pretty good reasoning. I can head back to my parents' house, but I'm thinking they probably wouldn't go there."

"Does Alonso have a favorite hangout? Is there a place the deaf kids just go to hang out?"

"The local pizza place over on Union Street or the arcade down on Church. Let's check the pizza place first."

"We also need to get in touch with Dylan's parents and let them know they need to contact us if he shows up at home."

Joseph wheeled the car toward the pizza place. Within

minutes, they were driving through the parking lot. "I don't see Alonso's or Dylan's car."

Catelyn sighed in disgust and shook her phone. "How long does it take to track a cell number?"

"If they're having to go through the cell carrier, it'll take a little bit. They're not at the arcade. I'm going to head toward the house."

"That seems like the last place they'd go."

"Do you have any better ideas?"

She heaved a sigh. "He's your brother."

"Right."

Catelyn leaned back and shut her eyes against the headache that was starting. Her phone buzzed, intruding on her brief moment of peace.

"Hello?"

"Catelyn, your target is somewhere on Sugarleaf Street. Um…704, to be specific."

"Thank, Bri."

She hung up. "They're at your parents' house. Or at least that's where Alonso's phone tracked to."

Joseph let a smug look briefly cross his face. She resisted the urge to punch him, decided to let him revel in his cleverness and sat back to finish the short ride while her adrenaline pumped at the thought of arresting Dylan.

Five minutes later, Joseph pulled into the driveway of his childhood home. They hopped out and made their way up the front porch and into the house. His mother greeted them, signing her welcome. "Joseph, what brings you here in the middle of the day? And Catelyn…" Surprise lifted her brows. "Hello, darling."

"Hi, Mrs. Santino."

Concerned flickered across her smooth, chubby face as she looked at Joseph. "What is it, son?"

"Is Alonso here, Mama?"

She twisted her ever present apron between her hands, then dropped it to sign, "No, he didn't come in the house. At least I didn't feel his usual thumping vibrations. He could have snuck in, I suppose. Is something wrong?"

Joseph told Catelyn, "I'll check his room. You explain to Mom what's going on."

"Okay."

He bounded up the stairs two at a time. Following the well-worn carpet to Alonso's room, he found the door open—and the room empty.

Just as he'd suspected.

Treading back down the steps, he found Catelyn and his mother deep in conversation. Ever since practically being adopted into his family, Catelyn had learned to sign on an expert level. As a CODA, Child of a Deaf Adult, Joseph had learned American Sign Language before he could speak.

He broke into the conversation. "He's not up there."

Confusion stamped plainly on her face, Catelyn turned to go back to the car. Joseph followed. She got in and got on the radio. Within seconds, she had Bri on the line. "Check the signal again, will you?"

A short wait. The radio squawked and Bri said, "Still the same location, Catelyn."

She turned to Joseph and said, "The phone's still here somewhere. The boys at least stopped by here. Do you think they could have left again with Alonso forgetting his phone—or leaving it behind on purpose?"

"Alonso wouldn't leave his phone. It's like an extension of his body."

"Unless he thought we might track him with it."

"I don't think he'd think about that, to be honest. He'd just be doing his best to get away to a place where he and Dylan could talk—or hide out."

"Then they're here. Somewhere." She rubbed her forehead. "I'd call the phone and see if it would ring, but no doubt it's on vibrate. I'm trying to think of some good hiding places from when we played hide-and-seek all those years ago."

"He's not in the house, I…" Joseph broke off and looked her in the eye. "Granny's suite."

"Excuse me?"

"The basement. I almost forgot all about it. Come on."

She scrambled from the car as he led the way to the side of the house. "It has a separate entrance and everything. We never use it, haven't used it in forever. It's been closed off since our grandmother died. With Alonso being the only kid left at home, Mom didn't need the space and didn't want to have to worry about cleaning it, so she just closed it down."

They reached the door. Catelyn looked down. "Footprints."

"Recent ones. Just the right size for a couple of teenage boys, too. See those prints there? They're different from the ones on this side."

"No use knocking, they're both deaf."

He twisted the knob and the door swung inward. "They didn't bother to lock the door." He stepped inside taking in the large area jam packed with antiques, family mementos and other unused, probably forgotten items.

A light snuffed out and darkness shrouded them. Joseph stated, "Yep, they're here."

"But they don't want us to know that they are."

"Back up."

"What?"

"Just do it, will you?"

Huffing a sigh, she did it. Joseph pulled the door shut as he exited.

"What are you doing now?" she demanded.

"Waiting. Now, you head around to the side and cover the window." Thunder rumbled and he looked at the sky. Gray clouds billowed overhead.

"Fine, what are we waiting on though?"

"One of them to check and see if the coast is clear. It'll save us hunting through that dusty mess and trying to chase down a scared kid. Let's just let them come to us."

Realization crossed her face.

"You're still a rat, Joseph."

"But a clever one, you must admit." Oh, how he loved it when the red flush took over and she looked at him in annoyance. But she couldn't help the small smile that tried to curve her lush lips.

"All right," she admitted, "a clever one." She left him and he watched her round the corner.

"Joseph?" she called. "They've already managed to get out. I can see them running. I'm going after them!"

"What? How?" He made his way around to find Catelyn racing off in the direction of the road.

Five minutes later, Catelyn leaned her palms against her knees and puffed, "Nice work, Colombo. Very clever."

"Hey, how was I supposed to know they'd move so fast? They ran up the stairs and out the back door. Mom's still shaking her fist at them."

"If we'd just gone in and…never mind. How far away could they be?"

"Far enough. There's tons of places to hide around here, and it's not a far hike into town to some of the stores."

"Then let's get officers here to set up a perimeter and a K-9 unit."

"We need a chopper, too."

Joseph was already talking into his radio. When he finished, he looked at her grim-faced and furious as he pulled out his BlackBerry.

"What are you doing?" she asked, annoyance still evident.

"Telling Alonso to haul himself back here and that he'd better hurry up and talk his friend into turning himself in."

"You think he'll listen?"

"There's always hope. He's been making some good decisions lately. Let's hope he adds this one to the list."

Catelyn sighed. "Running from the cops doesn't seem like a very good decision to me."

"You're right, it doesn't." He ran a hand through his hair. "I really think Alonso will come through. He's got a baseball game tonight. That is if it's not cancelled." He looked at the clouds that were threatening to release a downpour. "There's no way he'd jeopardize the team's status by not showing up. When he shows, I'll grab him and grill him, okay? And if it's cancelled, I'll figure something else out."

Indecision marred her features and he wanted to reach out and smooth her wrinkled forehead. Instead, he clenched his fingers into a fist. "Let's get in the car and see if we can track them down."

"Fine."

They hurried to his vehicle and he pulled the door open. A raindrop smacked his nose before he had a chance to duck inside.

Catelyn's door slammed and she pointed. "That way.

"Do you see them anywhere?" she asked as he circled the block.

Her question distracted him for a moment. "No, I'll try this other side street."

Catelyn watched him drive, competent, strong…intense. Swallowing hard, she refocused her attention on the search. She picked up the radio and called for backup in the neighborhood. Joseph sighed, but didn't protest. He wanted to find these kids as soon as possible, too.

The drizzle turned into a steady downpour.

"We're never going to be able to spot them in this mess. They've most likely holed up somewhere." He slapped the steering wheel, frustration stamped on his forehead.

"Let's get the dogs out. They can track anything, even in the rain."

"I'll call it in."

While he did that, she answered her ringing phone. Slapping it to her ear, she stared out her window at the rain. "Hello? What? When?" She whirled back around to look at him.

His gaze sharpened, and she knew he could see the worry on her face. "What is it?"

"I'll be right there." She hung up and bit her lip.

"What?" he insisted.

"My mother." Her voice shook. She cleared her throat. "She's taken a turn for the worse. They can't wake her up. She's…"

He stopped the car, then did a three-point turn. "I'll take you back to the station to get your car. You go see about your mother and I'll take care of the case—and Alonso. Call me as soon as you know something."

She hesitated, stared up at him like she wanted to say something.

"What is it?"

"Thank you, Joseph."

"For what?"

"Just…" She shrugged. "Thanks."

Five minutes later, he pulled up beside her car and placed

a hand on her arm. "I know you need to go, but…be thinking about what you want, Catelyn, okay? When all this is over, could we please sit down and have a major talk?" Intense brown eyes held her captive.

What she *wanted?* Have a major talk?

"What do you mean, Joseph? I want to solve this case. I want to find Kelly Franklin, I want…"

His finger covered her lips and she froze. "I mean—" his throat bobbed, betraying his cool, seemingly unaffected attitude "—is there a possibility for there to be an 'us' again? Could you possibly want to explore these feelings that are still there between us?"

Catelyn shut her mind against the instant rush of wonderful memories with this man, and instead, focused on the reason they'd split up.

"You're a cop."

His brown eyes glinted. She hadn't denied she still had feelings for him and he'd picked up on that. "I'll agree with that."

"Well, so am I. And I'm not giving that up."

"Did I ask you to?" Confusion flickered as he sat back to stare at her.

"Yes, Joseph, you did."

The stunned look on his face floored her. Did he not realize? "I told you about my father and you started acting just like him."

Stunned, he countered, "How did you come up with that? You said he wanted your mother to stay home and be mom and a wife. What's wrong with that?"

"Everything!"

How could anyone so smart be so dense?

She hopped out of his car and into hers, cranked the engine and sped off.

* * *

Women.

Joseph drove back to his parents' home with the vain hope that Alonso had come to his senses and returned there. The dogs would be here shortly to pick up the scent. Joseph would let them do their job while he did his.

Parking in the drive, he shook his head, opened the door and dashed through the rain into the house. *Having grown up in a household full of women, you'd think I would understand them by now, but I don't, God, especially not Catelyn. What did I say that was so wrong? So I would prefer that she think about staying home instead of working. Is that so wrong?*

Guilt gnawed at him as he thought about the conversations that seemed to come in spurts. He'd never asked her to quit being cop.

Not in so many words.

But what did his actions say? Was he *not* saying something that he should put into words?

But what? How could he reassure her that they could work everything out? What did she need to hear to put her fears to rest?

Lost in thought, he intended to make his way to the back bedroom, the one across from his parents' master bedroom, but his mother stepped out of the kitchen cutting off his path. "Is everything all right?" she signed.

Not wanting to worry her, he signed back, "I think it will be. Nothing for you to be anxious about, okay?"

She waved aside his words then planted her hands on ample hips before lifting them one more time to sign. "I may not be a big bad FBI agent, but I'm still a mother and I know when something's wrong." Narrowing her eyes, she signed, "If you don't want to tell me, fine, but don't try to tell me everything's all right when your face, the tension in your shoulders and your heavy footsteps tell me another story."

"Mom, I'm sorry." He tamped down his impatience to get moving. "No, everything's not all right, but I don't want to say anything right now. There, is that better?"

"Much." She stood on tiptoes while he bent at the waist. She pressed a kiss to his cheek then she reached up to pat it with a soft hand. "You need to shave. Your father and I are going out to eat with friends. Alonso's game has been canceled due to the rain. You're welcome to join us or eat the casserole in the fridge."

"I'll take the casserole, thanks." He backed toward his room, needing to get going.

"I think we're going to go see one of the late movies after we eat, so don't worry about us if we're not home until midnight or so, okay?"

She headed back into the kitchen to grab her purse, and Joseph bolted for his room.

Even as he kept an eye out for the K-9 unit, love for his mother filled him. He heard his dad's footsteps heading in the direction of Joseph's mom. All his life, his mother had been a living example of the kind of woman Joseph wanted to marry.

Without warning, Catelyn's pretty features flashed into his mind. Ruthlessly, he shoved them away. Catelyn had made it clear she wasn't interested in marrying a cop. And, too late, he'd discovered she wasn't interested in being a stay-at-home wife and mother, which is the kind of woman he'd always pictured himself settling down with. The thought of marrying a career woman had never held any appeal for him. Call him old-fashioned, but that was just the way he was. And the thought of Catelyn being hurt or killed was just more than he could bear. His heart cramped at the thought. But he'd figured they'd work through it. Find a solution, a compromise that would make them both happy. However, before he could even present the idea to her, she'd refused to see him, have anything to do with him. So when he got the call from New York saying the FBI job was his if he wanted it, he'd taken it.

Maybe he should have pushed harder to get her to talk to him, but…he'd been hurt, too. So, he'd left.

Only now he had regrets. Lots of them. And he'd come to realize a future with Catelyn would be completely different than what he'd always pictured. She didn't meet any of the expectations he'd mentally placed on his future spouse; add in Catelyn's reserve about marrying another officer and he had hurdles in his path that he didn't know if he could successfully leap over.

And he wasn't interested in a job change. Although, if it meant doing it for her…

Was he willing to revamp everything he'd ever thought about when it came to marriage and family?

He sighed and focused his attention back to the case. He simply had to put Catelyn and their relationship out of his mind until this case was over. So he turned his thoughts to his brother.

He heard his parents leave. Two minutes later, the unit arrived. Grabbing Alonso's pillow from his bed, he carried it downstairs to meet the handler, Christine Palmer and her K-9, Zorro.

"Hey, Christine, how are you?"

The petite redhead nodded at him. "Doing well, Joseph. Good to see you again."

"Yeah, you too. I just wish it wasn't for this reason." He held the pillow out to the German shepherd at her side. The dog took a good sniff and Christine put him to work.

"Let me know immediately what you find, will you?" he

hollered at her disappearing back. "I'll be right here working on what I can from this end."

"You got it," she yelled.

Worry about Alonso engulfed him. His suspicion that the game would be cancelled had come to fruition. That meant Alonso was out there somewhere. With a BOLO out on both boys, it wouldn't be long before he would be getting a phone call that they'd been picked up. His heart ached at the thought of his brother's involvement. He just hoped it didn't come to the point where he had to excuse himself from the case.

He still had a couple of hours before darkness would fall.

He pulled out his laptop and connected to his parents' wireless server. Then ran a specialized software program that would ensure privacy while he used the Internet.

For an hour or so, he worked, running another background check on all the individuals involved in the case. There was nothing on any of the teenagers except Dylan Carlisle. The boy had been arrested as a juvenile for shoplifting, minor vandalism, joyriding without a license—and assault and battery.

Old news.

His phone rang. He grabbed it before the sound faded. "Hello?"

"Joseph? This is Christine. The dog tracked the scent down the road a bit, then I think the boys got into a car because Zorro completely lost them."

Great. He sighed. "Thanks. Give Zorro an extra treat from me."

"Sure thing."

So now he would wait and see if an officer picked them up. Who would have given them a ride? A question Alonso would answer just as soon as Joseph caught up with him.

A little more research into Dylan's background showed the assault and battery was a school fight. The charges on that had later been dropped. He'd had a shoplifting charge and served some community service for the shoplifting charge. Other than that, the kid really didn't have a record.

Still, it didn't look good for the boy.

And yet, Alonso obviously believed in his friend enough to help him at the risk of some major trouble for himself.

Another hour flew by before his stomach growled, reminding him he needed to eat something. Time had passed quickly with Joseph so engrossed in what he was doing, he hadn't noticed the sun going down.

His phone rang.

Catelyn.

He picked it up on the second ring. "Hello?"

"Have you found the boys yet?" She didn't waste any time getting to the point, did she?

"Not yet. The K-9 unit came out, but the boys must have gotten into a car because the dog lost them. I'm trying to decide the next step in this case. I traced Alonso's cell phone again and got nothing. I think he's pulled the battery out. Same with Dylan's. I finally got ahold of Dylan's mother and she gave me the number."

"Great. Well, look, I'm almost home. I need to pick up something to take back to my mother, then I can meet you somewhere. Back at the office or wherever, or we can try to find Alonso and Dylan again."

"Fine, give me a call when you're ready. I'll keep working it from this angle. How's your mom?"

"She had an allergic reaction to something she ate, but she's doing better, thanks. I'll call you shortly, okay?"

"Sounds good."

She hung up, and Joseph just sat there for a moment trying to figure the woman out. He looked back at the computer and then realized how dark the room had become.

Squinting through the blackness, he reached for the switch on the bedside table when the floor creaked under the weight of a footstep.

He froze. Listened.

Another creak. Like a person shifting his weight.

Alonso? No, that kid would burst into Joseph's room unannounced with no hesitation—at least he would've before today.

Whoever it was, he—or she—was standing just outside the bedroom door, making no attempt to knock or announce himself. Could it be his dad?

Probably not. Engrossed in his work, Joseph's mind had absently registered the sound of the door closing behind his parents when they'd left the house hours ago.

Not wanting to call out and let the person know Joseph knew someone was outside his door, he eased his way over to the drawer of his nightstand, slid it open and wrapped his fingers around his gun.

Could it be Alonso after all? Trying to work up the courage to face his brother?

Or someone with a more sinister motive in mind?

Catelyn drove toward home, her mind in a jumble. Her mother was fine. A false alarm. The allergic reaction had been resolved with a whopping dose of Benadryl. As a result, the poor woman had just been too tired to bother to respond to those trying to wake her.

Catelyn stayed as long as she felt necessary. When her mother had awakened long enough to look at her with that blank expression on her face, Catelyn's heart nearly broke and she knew it wouldn't matter if she stayed or left. On her way out, a nurse stopped her and asked, "Do you know what your mother may have meant by the words *fun album*?"

Confused, Catelyn thought. "No, why?"

"She was asking for it earlier. Wanted her fun album."

"Um…no, not really. I can't think of what she might have…" Realization dawned. "Wait a minute. I might know what she's talking about after all. I have a photo album at home. It has pictures in it of the one time we actually took a family vacation."

"Could you bring it next time you come?"

"I'll bring it back tonight."

"Oh, but you don't have to…"

But Catelyn was already out the door. If her mother wanted that album tonight, she'd have it.

Her stomach growled reminding her she hadn't eaten in a while. If she waited too much longer, she'd get the shakes. As she drove past the grocery store nearest her house, she recognized a car in the parking lot.

Sandy.

On impulse, she spun into the lot and parked still thinking about her continued interaction with Joseph.

Why on earth did *that man* still have an effect on her emotions, her heart, her—everything? It made no sense.

Lord, I gave him up two years ago. I told You I would dedicate my life to You and serve You in the capacity of being the best cop I could be. What purpose do You have in bringing Joseph back into my life?

Anger stirred beneath the surface. What right did he have to come back and interfere? Acting like everything should be all right between them? Wanting to talk about "us"?

"Hi. Catelyn."

Startled, she turned at the sound of her name. Just the person she'd been looking for.

"Oh, hi. Sandy. How are you doing?"

"Fine thanks. Just taking a little break from work to grab a few of the necessities. My cupboard is looking a little bare."

Catelyn gave a small laugh. "I know what you mean."

"How's the case progressing?" Sandy tossed a pack of chocolate chip cookies into her cart.

Catelyn grabbed a ready-made roast beef sandwich and a bag of chips. She grimaced and shook her head. "Actually, I saw your car in the parking lot and thought I'd come hunt you down. I was going to ask you the same question. Unfortunately, it seems like we're spinning our wheels on this end. Although, if I could go without sleeping or eating, I might have it solved by now."

"Well, I don't have anything from the lab for you yet, sorry."

Shrugging, Catelyn stepped into the line to pay for her sandwich. "It's all right. I know you'll call when you do, I just decided to stop…" She paused.

The woman offered a commiserating smile. "So…you're working with Joseph Santino?"

Catelyn might have known this subject would come up. Taking a deep breath, she nodded sighed, and handed her sandwich and chips to the cashier as she dug in her front pocket for a ten-dollar bill. "Yes, I am."

"How's that going?"

Sandy knew the history there. She'd been there with a shoulder for Catelyn to cry on two years ago. "It's definitely interesting."

Sympathy flashed on her friend's face. "Well, if you need me, you know where to find me."

"Yeah, the lab. You work too hard."

"Isn't that the pot calling the kettle black?"

Catelyn grimaced. "I suppose it is. And thanks for the offer. Actually, to be honest, I'm not sure what's going on. The feelings are still there—on both sides. I'm just…"

"Scared of getting hurt again?"

"Right. Thanks for beating around the bush."

"Well, it's no wonder. I don't blame you. But I think you're dumb if you let him get away again. He's not like your dad."

Catelyn blinked at the woman's directness. "Maybe not, but I'm afraid I might be too much like my mom."

"There is that. But you need to keep one thing in mind."

"What's that?"

"I don't know Joseph very well. Just what I've heard. But I do know he's highly respected and lives his faith. You do, too."

Confused where she was going with this, Catelyn wrinkled her brow and waited.

Sandy didn't disappoint her. "You and Joseph are both believers. You love God. Your parents didn't have that."

Stunned, Catelyn could only stare at Sandy as she processed that statement. Then looked at the cashier. The woman patiently waited for Catelyn to pay. Catelyn handed over the money with an embarrassed shrug.

Sandy smiled sympathetically. "I'll see you later. Take care and let me know how it works out. I'll be praying for you guys. And I'll also let you know as soon as I have something from the lab."

Pulling into her driveway ten minutes later, Catelyn realized with a start she had no memory of the drive home. Great.

Climbing out of the car, she grabbed her sandwich from the seat beside her. At least it had finally quit raining.

Her empty house loomed in the evening light. Soon it would be completely dark. And she would be alone once more. Normally, she didn't mind the solitude, but now that Joseph had come back, she found herself longing for his company once again.

And that just wouldn't do. She'd fallen for him once, then learned he expected her to quit her job to stay home and be his dutiful little wife.

Catelyn shuddered, grateful she'd found that out before she

married him. She would have been her mother all over again, living a life of misery, full of arguments and…

Nausea churned in her as she shut down that line of linking. What a disaster that would have been.

She sat there for a moment, considering whether or not to eat her sandwich right there or take it inside.

Inside might be better. She could grab the album then get back into the car to make the drive back to the nursing home before she hooked back up with Joseph to continue working on the case. If she just sat here, she'd keep thinking about Joseph.

Climbing out of her car, she unwrapped the sandwich and took a bite. She needed to hurry. Kelly was still missing; Alonso and Dylan needed to be found. She had no time to waste and felt a little guilty for stopping to eat when so much needed to be done. And Joseph would be waiting for her call.

Joseph. She stomped up the steps of her front porch. He should have just stayed in New York. But he hadn't. He'd come back. True, it wasn't because he'd opted to do so. It was because of a case, but he was back and she wanted him to stay.

Really, really wanted him to stay.

With her.

Exasperated with herself for her inability to purge him from her thoughts, she grabbed her key, inserted it and turned it to the right.

And stopped.

There had been no familiar click.

Her door hadn't been locked.

Shut, but not locked.

Had she forgotten when she'd left for work this morning? Not likely.

With careful, watchful movements, Catelyn unsnapped the strap holding her gun in the holster just under her armpit. Pulling the weapon out, she stepped just inside the door.

Did she have an intruder, and was he still here?

The brief thought that she should call for backup flittered through her mind. But if she'd simply forgotten to lock the door, she'd feel pretty silly calling this in. She'd never live it down.

Not that she should let pride get in the way of safety, still…

The small foyer curved around into the den.

Again, she came to an abrupt halt.

It had been trashed. In one sweeping glance, she took in the destruction. Her television sported a gaping a hole, jagged glass grinning at her like an evil jack-o'-lantern. It looked like it had been wantonly smashed with a blunt object. The rest of her electronics were gone, bare spaces on her entertainment center mocking her.

Shock and revulsion filled her. Not that the scene was anything new. She dealt with this kind of thing every day. Only now, it had happened to her.

She found it chilling. Horrific.

Scary.

Backing out of the room, she reached for her cell phone. She needed help.

That's when she heard the running feet coming up behind her.

SIX

Joseph swung the gun up, keeping the nose pointed toward the threat that could possibly be waiting on the other side of the door. Sliding his feet out of his shoes, he crept toward the door.

Positioning himself to the side, he waited.

Listened.

Heard nothing.

Then a scrape, like the shuffle of a foot. And his mom thought his shoulders had been tense before. The muscles across the base of his neck felt ready to snap.

With his left hand, he reached for the knob.

Before he could get a good grip, he felt it turning under his palm.

Pulling his hand away like he'd touched a hot stove, he raised it to join his right hand, wrapping his fingers around the butt of the gun in a two-hand hold.

He stepped back so that he was an arm's length away from the door. Just the right distance between him and the head of the person who entered.

Light filtered from the attached bathroom opposite the wall where he stood. The faint glow enabled him to see the knob turning. Instead of watching it finish its journey around, he raised his eyes and brought his arms down to aim the weapon at head level.

And waited.

Slowly, the door opened. The hinges squeaked and the person on the other side paused.

And waited.

Breathing coming more shallowly, Joseph felt his adrenaline surging, could feel his heart pounding. But his cool professionalism never wavered.

Who was it?

Catelyn whirled to confront her intruder and got a glimpse of a ski mask before the person rammed into her, knocking her back against the foyer wall. Her feet went out from under her and she landed on her backside.

With a whoosh, her breath left her; her gun flew from her fingers and skittered across the hardwoods.

Pounding feet moved in the direction of the front door.

Oh, no you don't, you little punk.

From her sprawled position on the floor, lungs still screaming for a deep breath, she threw out a foot and connected with a shin of the escaping thug.

"Ah!" He went down.

But before she could react, he threw a punch in her direction. It caught her on the cheek, snapping her head back against the floor.

Stars danced in front of her eyes.

No time to pass out. Get the gun.

Shaking off the dizziness and a sudden wave of nausea, she scrambled toward the weapon. More pounding feet. The slam of the door and her aching head left her ears ringing.

She reached for her cell phone and punched in the direct

work line to her friend, a dispatcher for the 911 service here in Spartanburg.

"911. What's your emergency?"

"Hey, Tara, it's Catelyn," She winced at the breathy sound of her voice and cleared her throat.

"Catelyn? Are you okay?"

"Ah, no, not really. My home was broken into and I surprised the creeps."

"I'm dispatching a unit right now." The familiar, friendly tone in her voice disappeared as she turned into the skilled professional she'd been for seven years. "Do you need an ambulance? Are you hurt?"

"No, not too bad."

"That means you're hurt. You get an ambulance."

"No, no, seriously, I think I'm all right. Just a few knocks and bruises. It could have been a lot worse."

"Just stay on the line with me."

Catelyn did because she knew if she didn't she'd wind up with more than just a police cruiser in her driveway. Vaguely, she registered Tara's dispatch speech, the codes she used and knew the woman was sending an ambulance whether Catelyn wanted one or not.

She just hoped Joseph wasn't in his car listening to the scanner.

Joseph kept the gun steady. The door continued its inward swing to land on the opposite wall from Joseph. As soon as the figure stepped inside, Joseph placed the gun against his head.

The person froze.

And thanks to the moonlight, Joseph got a good look at his intruder.

Dylan.

Joseph quickly pointed the gun elsewhere and flipped on the

light switch. The boy's eyes were wide and scared, his hands held out from his body.

Signing with one hand, Joseph demanded, "What do you think you're doing, sneaking into someone's house, Dylan? Not smart."

"I need help."

"You bet you do. Go in the den while I put this away." Joseph made sure the safety was on, but slipped it into the waistband of his pants. He believed Dylan was innocent, and yet…

Exiting the room, he made his way into the den where he found Dylan sitting on the couch chewing a thumbnail to the quick.

Sighing, Joseph signed, "Why'd you run, Dylan? And why are sneaking around this house? That's a pretty good way to get yourself shot."

The boy threw his hands up and signed back, "I was scared. I don't want to go to jail. I didn't kill Tracy, but nobody believes me." He swallowed hard. "Actually, I did knock, but when you didn't answer, I decided to come find you. I didn't want to leave because I was scared someone else might be looking for me and you're the only one who even thinks it's possible that I might be innocent."

Had he been that into what he was doing that he hadn't heard the knock on the door? Must have been. "You should have rung the bell," he grumbled. "Did you know there's a warrant out for your arrest?"

Dylan's throat bobbed again in time with the jerky nod of his head. His right hand curled into a fist that he shook with the sign for "Yes." "I know. I saw the teachers talking about it in the office. They didn't know I'd come down there to turn in some papers. They were saying that you were on the way to arrest me."

"So you ran." A statement.

Dylan nodded.

"And got my brother in the middle of it. What kind of friend does that?"

Tears gathered in Dylan's eyes and Joseph hated to be so harsh, but the kid needed to realize the seriousness of his situation.

Dylan nodded, signing, "I know. That's why when Alonso insisted I come find you, I had to do it."

"He insisted, huh? Where is Alonso anyway?"

"He's waiting on the porch. He said I had to do this. Turn myself in and let you see that I'm not guilty. That I'm willing to let you help prove that I'm not a killer. So, will you help me?"

Joseph stood and strode through the room, into the foyer and opened the door. His brother sat on the two-seater swing, rocking like he hadn't a care in the world. He looked up when Joseph appeared in the doorway to sign. "Get yourself in here, little brother."

A frown marred the teen's forehead, but he didn't argue, just rose and followed Joseph back into the house.

Once in the den, Alonso looked at Dylan and signed, "Well, did you ask him?"

"Yes."

Joseph looked back and forth between the two. He signed to Alonso, "So you convinced him to turn himself in."

"Yeah. Running was stupid and I told him that. I also told him that you would prove he didn't kill Tracy or hurt Kelly but he had to turn himself in."

The weight of his younger brother's unwavering faith fell heavily on Joseph's shoulders. "You told him that, huh?"

Alonso shrugged, signing, "Sure, it's what you do and as you're always saying, it's what you do well, so why wouldn't you be able to help my friend out?"

Joseph paced from one end of the room to the other, then turned to face his brother and sign, "All right, Mom and Dad went to the late movie after supper. I want to get this taken care of before they get back. So, here's what we're going to do. I'm going to call Detective Clark and let her know that I'm arresting you, all right?"

Dylan's eyes went huge, but he didn't say anything. Joseph continued, keeping his signs fluid, "You may have to spend some time behind bars, but I've got friends in the system and can probably get you in a cell by yourself, all right? So no one would bother you. It'll buy us time to find out who's behind all this, okay?"

Some of the fear left Dylan at Joseph's reassurances. Being deaf, the kid would be terrified to be in a place where communication would be limited. Not that there weren't other deaf inmates, but the majority of them were adults. No way was Joseph letting this kid be subjected to that if he could help it. "Who gave you a ride when you ran from here earlier?"

"Chad drove by and we hopped in."

"Chad, huh? I thought he was mad at Dylan."

"Naw, they made up. After he calmed down and he and Dylan talked about it, he doesn't think Dylan had anything to do with killing Tracy any more than I do."

"Why wasn't he in school?"

Alonso flushed. Joseph answered for him. "Skipping, huh?"

His brother offered a shrug and looked away.

Joseph picked up his BlackBerry and punched the number he had on speed dial for Catelyn.

Officers crowded her small cottage-style house. The two-bedroom, two bath home glowed brighter than a Christmas tree on December 25.

Neighbors peered out windows, some stepped out onto their

porches, and Catelyn knew she'd be the recipient of more casseroles and desserts than she'd be able to eat over the next few days. Not that her neighbors didn't genuinely like her and visit occasionally, but Catelyn had a feeling visits would triple. They were good people, just a nosy bunch.

Paramedics and medical personnel swarmed her and she fought them off claiming she was fine. They insisted on bandaging the cut on her cheek. She let them just to get them off her back. Itching to get back in and help the crime-scene guys process her den, she finally pushed the good-intentioned hands away and hopped off the back of the ambulance. "Thanks, guys."

Before stepping through the door, she scanned the front of her house and driveway. Four police cars sat outside her home. "I only wanted one unit," she muttered under her breath.

And yet, she was secretly touched. They'd heard about one of their own being in trouble and had immediately responded. Couldn't ask for more than that.

Sighing, she braced herself and went inside. Silently, she surveyed the mess. Then heard her phone ringing—somewhere. Where had she left it? Looking around, she spotted her purse on the table just inside the foyer by the door. Oh, right. Grabbing the bag, she fished the phone out and answered it on the last ring.

"Hello."

"Catelyn?"

"Joseph?"

"Yeah. You busy?"

She looked around and gave a small laugh devoid of humor. "Um, a little bit, yes. Can I call you back in a couple of hours? Oh, wait a minute, what time is it?"

"It's around eight-thirty, I think. I just wanted to let you know I've got Dylan Carlisle here my house. I'm placing him under arrest. You want to meet me at the station or come here?"

The floor shifted beneath her feet. "Excuse me? Did you just say you had Dylan Carlisle?"

"Nothing wrong with *your* hearing, is there?"

"Um, okay, right. It's just I'm a little busy. Someone broke into my house and I'm dealing with the aftermath."

"What?!"

She winced and pulled the phone away from her ear. "Nothing wrong with my hearing, remember?"

"Are you okay?" he demanded.

She was so tired of telling people she was fine. "I'm fine. I'll be there in a few minutes."

"You got it. We'll be waiting on you."

Ten minutes later, Catelyn finished giving her statement and once again assuring everyone she suffered no serious side effects of her run-in with the attacker.

Finally, the crime-scene guys packed it in. Sarah Hinson, part of the CSU team, stopped her as she rushed for the door. "We'll check out the prints and stuff, but I'll tell you right now, this is looking similar to the break-ins going on over on the west side of town."

"I've heard about those, heard the chatter in the office, but haven't really kept up with what's happening."

"Whoever's involved is getting bold. They broke into a home with the owners there."

Concern pinched her. "Was anyone hurt?"

"Nope, the old man was asleep on the couch. His wife was downstairs in the basement in their home office. Perps walked in an unlocked door and started hauling stuff away. Started in the bedrooms and worked their way forward. By the time the guy woke up and realized someone was in his house, it was too late. They ran, climbed into a waiting van and took off. The guy just said it was a nondescript blue van. Didn't even get a license plate because he didn't have his glasses on."

"Scary." And it was. "Look, I've got to run. Thanks for all your help."

"Just doing my job. Take care of that head of yours."

Wincing, Catelyn raised a hand to touch the knot at the base of her skull. Her cheek throbbed, too. "I will."

She picked up the album that had fallen to the floor and placed it on the small table to the left of her front door. Her mother would just have to wait. She had a murderer to put behind bars.

Joseph heard her car pull into the driveway and let the boys know Catelyn had arrived. Dylan immediately lost what little relaxation he'd managed to achieve. Alonso blew out a sigh between pursed lips and eyed his friend.

When the knock came at the door, Joseph crossed the room to open it. She entered, her gaze zeroing in on Dylan. Seeing his slumped, dejected form, she stopped. For a brief moment, she looked like she'd rather be anywhere else; doing anything other than what she'd sworn to do.

Uphold the law.

"Catie." Joseph breathed as he took in her bruised cheek and disheveled appearance.

She held up a hand. "I'm fine."

Then she straightened her shoulders and marched into the den, signing, "Get up, Dylan, and let's go. I suppose Joseph's already read you your rights." At his affirming nod, she signed as she talked, explaining that the DNA on the ring had come back matching Dylan's. He raised a hand to his chin. To the cut Joseph had noticed his first day back. The cut he'd just figured had been a result of shaving.

Hesitantly, fear radiating off him in waves, Dylan rose and held out his hands. Catelyn efficiently snapped them into place and signed, "Let's go."

Joseph frowned at her brusqueness. Normally, in a situation on the street, he wouldn't have thought twice about it, but here in his parents' living room with a scared kid who'd just turned himself in, she seemed so…uncaring.

It hurt to watch. The Catelyn he'd known two years ago would've…no, he couldn't think about that. At least she'd cuffed the kid's hands in front of him so he could still communicate. Joseph turned to Alonso and signed, "I'll be back. Tell Mom and Dad what's going on when they get back, all right?"

He followed her to the squad car. An unmarked, beige Town Car that shouted "Cop." Dylan obediently allowed Catelyn to herd him into the car.

Joseph settled into the passenger seat. He noticed she didn't offer him the keys. "You've changed."

Cranking the car, she ignored his statement. At least that's what it looked like to him. They drove in complete silence to the jail. Things didn't improve as they walked inside to the booking area.

Joseph cleared his throat. "I called his parents while we were waiting for you. They should be here somewhere. At least his mother will. You never know with his dad."

She didn't even blink, just nodded. "An interpreter is on the way."

Even though he and Catelyn were both highly skilled in ASL, it would be a conflict of interest for either of them to act in the capacity of interpreter.

Twenty minutes later, Jonathan Wise arrived and jumped into his job with skilled professionalism. Dylan knew the man from the deaf school and seemed relieved, if a little embarrassed to see him. Dylan's mother arrived shortly after the booking process began.

The interpreter explained to Dylan that he would have a hearing within seventy-two hours. Dylan shrugged. He'd been through this before, but had never been charged with something so serious. Once booked, Joseph led him to an interrogation room, the interpreter dutifully following.

Once in the interrogation room, Catelyn stood against the wall while Joseph sat down opposite of Dylan. The teen's mother waited in another area and his lawyer was on the way.

Staring at Catelyn, he wondered at the expression on her face. Tense, resolute. Poor Dylan.

The door opened and a heavyset woman in her mid fifties entered the room. "I'm Rose Donovan, Dylan's lawyer."

After handshakes all around, the lawyer and her client faced off the Special Agent and the Homicide Detective.

Here goes round one, thought Joseph.

"Now, what's my client being charged with?"

Catelyn sucked in a deep breath and repeated everything she'd told Dylan when he'd been arrested. The interpreter didn't miss a thing.

"Now," Catelyn concluded, "Jocelyn's already read Dylan his rights, the interpreter was there and we've got it on camera. He understands everything." She passed the paper to the lawyer who tapped it and nodded. "The big question tonight is why Dylan's DNA was on Tracy's ring when he claims he never saw her that night."

The boy signed. "All right. Here's the truth. The rest of it anyway."

So, he had been holding back. Joseph felt anger twist his insides. "You should have come clean long before now, Dylan."

Defiance flashed for a brief moment, then he dropped his eyes to the table. When he raised them to Joseph, he asked, "Just wait until I tell you everything before you get all mad." Another deep breath. "I didn't kill Tracy, so I didn't think it would matter."

Catelyn stomped to the table, leaned over and growled as

she signed, "Spill. And if you leave out a single, solitary detail, I'll nail your hide to the wall, do you understand me?"

Dylan recoiled, his own anger bubbling just below the surface. Joseph could see it clearly.

"Catelyn, back off a little, huh?"

She whirled. "Don't tell me how to do my job."

Whoa. Her eyes snapped a clear warning. He held up both hands in the universal gesture for surrender. "Fine."

She gritted, "Thanks." Turning back to Dylan, she took a deep breath. "Go ahead."

Catelyn felt the raging anger deep down inside. Anger at Dylan, anger at herself for being a sucker once more, anger at Joseph for butting in and coming home. And anger at God.

Her knees nearly buckled at the realization. Stiffening her spine, she made sure none of her emotions showed on her face. Professionalism in its purest form radiated from her. She'd deal with this newfound self-awareness later.

Dylan started signing. "Yes, I was there with Kelly, just like I told you before. But —" his signs slowed "—Tracy was there, too."

Catelyn blew out an annoyed breath. Dylan didn't notice but Joseph shot her a look. She ignored it "Go on."

"When I walked up to meet Kelly, she and Tracy were arguing. I only caught part of the conversation, but what I understood was that Tracy wanted Kelly to get involved in something and Kelly didn't want to."

"What was she trying to get Kelly involved in?"

"I'm not sure."

"But you have an idea?" This question came from Joseph. The lawyer's sharp eyes missed nothing and Catelyn knew she'd stop her client if it even looked like he was going to say something to incriminate himself.

Dylan nodded. "I think Tracy was trying to get Kelly to join The Skulls. The gang. It's getting really popular, growing by pretty big numbers."

"But Kelly didn't want to?" Catelyn furrowed a brow, concentrating hard.

"No. She thinks gangs are stupid. She and Billy both do. They're more into the church scene, not the criminal stuff." With a sense of relief, Catelyn took note of Dylan's use of the present tense when he talked about Kelly. If he did know where she was, he just told them that she was still alive.

If he knew where she was.

"Anyway, I asked her what they were arguing about and she refused to tell me. Tracy started yelling at me about staying out of her business and told me what a loser I was." He swallowed at the memory and wiped a hand across his lips, closing his eyes for a brief moment.

Catelyn and Joseph shared a look. And waited.

"Kelly got mad—" Dylan opened his eyes and finally signed, "At Tracy. She lost her temper and told Tracy she was done with their friendship, that blackmail was really low, but if she ever got her life straightened out or if she ever needed any help, Tracy could count on her to help, but if she kept doing the stuff she was doing, then they were done as friends."

"Wow, that's pretty heavy stuff," Joseph empathized. "Blackmail, huh?"

Dylan nodded, then stared at the table as though gathering his thoughts.

Catelyn leaned in, not bothering to hide the ire she felt. "Wait a minute, Dylan, you didn't mention the blackmail issue before. You didn't think that was important?"

He dropped his eyes from hers. "I didn't actually remember it until just now."

She tapped his hand and his eyes rose to meet hers. "Do you know who she was blackmailing?"

Keeping his gaze locked with hers, he signed, "No, I promise. I don't have a clue who she'd be blackmailing." He ran his fingers over his eyes, rubbed the bridge of his nose and signed, "Kelly was wearing my jacket. I'd given it to her earlier that day at school. When we turned to leave, Tracy grabbed the back of the jacket and jerked. Kelly's arms pulled back and the jacket slipped off. Tracy gave it a toss—" he mimicked the move like he was flinging something aside "—and when Kelly stumbled, Tracy pushed her to the ground."

"And you came to Kelly's defense, didn't you?" Joseph signed and asked the question at the same time, his voice soft, his signs slow. The interpreter mimicked his movements for the camera.

Dylan looked miserable. "Yeah, I did. When Kelly fell, Tracy went after her and lifted her foot like she was going to kick her right there on the ground." He looked around the table. "I couldn't just let her do that. I grabbed Tracy to pull her away from Kelly."

"So you pushed her?"

He gave a shake of his head. "No. I just grabbed her arm and pulled. That's when her hand flew back and her ring…" Fingers touched the healing spot on his chin.

Understanding crossed Joseph's face and he gave her another look. She kept her gaze on Dylan. "Then what?"

"I let go and told Kelly to come on. She refused. I begged her and she said she had unfinished business and wanted me to leave. I started to argue with her, but she was getting mad, yelled at me to go away, so…I left. I don't know what happened after that."

Startled at the abrupt ending to the story, Catelyn sat back with a thump. "That's it?"

Dylan shrugged. "That's it. That's why I didn't say anything about being there. I don't know what happened after I left," he reiterated. "I didn't think it was important. I didn't think anyone would believe me. I just…"

Catelyn stared at him as he trailed off. He met her gaze, then dropped it to the table. Did she believe him?

Joseph did, she could see it written all over him. And she trusted Joseph's judgment although she gave him a hard time sometimes. Frustration gnawed on her insides. Blackmail. That put a new twist on things.

Who was Tracy blackmailing and what kind of information did she have on that person?

Glancing at her watch, she saw that it was pushing 11:00. "Joseph, do you have any more questions?"

He looked surprised at her inquiry, like it shocked him that she'd bother to include him. Hurt bit her heart. Did he really think she was that hard-nosed? That she didn't respect him as a professional?

Well, it's not like you've been the most cooperative person in this partnership, her conscience sniped at her. Shame filled her and she avoided his gaze by watching Dylan's lawyer gather her stuff.

Joseph nodded. "I've got two questions. What was the relationship between Tracy and Zachary?"

"They were brother and sister."

"We know that," Joseph said patiently. "But did they get along? Hang out? That kind of stuff."

"No, they didn't like each other much. I mean, they did and they didn't. When Zachary did what Tracy wanted, they got along fine, but Zachary wanted out of the gang. He said something about coming into some cash and didn't need the gang anymore."

"Wait a minute. Do you know what he meant by that?"

"No, I never saw him with any big amount of money. Anyway, Tracy didn't want him to try and leave and was pushing him to stay in, calling him names and stuff, bullying him about being weak." He twisted his fingers. "I think she was scared that if Zachary tried to leave, the gang members would come after her and make an example of her. I don't know if that's what happened or not, but it wouldn't surprise me."

Joseph made a notation in his notebook. Catelyn felt her mind whirl with this new information. Then Joseph signed his last question. "Dylan, where did you go when you left Kelly?"

The boy paused then signed, "I just drove around, went downtown and watched the people coming and going from the bars, wishing I was old enough to go in."

"So there's no one who can vouch for you at the time of the murder?"

Dylan shook his head then dropped it into his hands. His shoulders shook as he sobbed.

Catelyn turned and left the room.

SEVEN

Joseph reassured Dylan once more that he would do everything in his power to prove his innocence and to just hang in there.

Then he went after Catelyn.

Locating her was easy. Out in the parking lot, she stood facing her car. Unmoving, still as stone.

When he placed a hand on her shoulder, she flinched, whirling to face him. "You said I've changed. What made you say that?"

He didn't answer right away. Instead, he suggested, "Why don't you take me home? We'll talk on the way."

She gave a short nod and pressed the keyless remote to unlock the doors. Silence filled the car for the first few minutes of the drive as he pondered how to word what he wanted to say, then he took a deep breath and ventured, "When I said you'd changed, I meant you're different. You were so…emotionless when we brought Dylan in. I don't remember that about you. You seem to have a new…hardness about you. Where's your compassion? The deep caring that you used to express for each and every person you come in contact with? The belief that everyone was innocent until proven guilty?"

Shocked, she stared at him for a full five seconds before swinging her eyes back to the road.

More silence as several miles clipped past.

Uh-oh. Had he done it now? Pushed her completely away?

He saw her shoulders lift as she breathed deep. But she still didn't respond. He gave her a couple of more minutes and right before she pulled into his driveway, he asked, "Catie?"

Staring straight ahead, she told him, "Just get out, Joseph."

"So, you're going to push me away again?"

Whiplike she faced him. That's when he saw the tears trembling on her lashes. "You left me! You left, packed up and moved away before…"

"Before what, Catie?" Her pain seared him, but maybe now they could find the answers they'd left in limbo two years ago. "You told me to leave, if I remember correctly. You said you couldn't ever be what I wanted, and that you needed space and time, that you didn't know if you'd ever be ready for marriage, especially to another cop. Is any of this ringing a bell?"

He should have left that last part off. But she didn't blast him on it. Her shoulders shook, and in the moonlight, he could see the tears fall. "But you weren't supposed to just…go. You lay out these expectations about how you want a wife like your mother—" she paused, thinking "—and I didn't want to quit my job."

She stopped, her frustration evident.

"I never asked you to quit your job!"

Catelyn realized she was losing the battle against the storm of tears threatening to unleash itself. "Yes, you did! I can't talk about this now, Joseph."

He opened his door and Catelyn stared in shock as he slammed it. Then he marched around to the driver's side, unbuckled her seat belt and pulled her out of her seat. "Hey!"

"Come on."

"What are doing?" she protested, but didn't fight him.

"What I should have done two years ago."

He led her through the front yard, around to the back and down to the little pond that sat on the edge of his parents' property.

His touch turned gentle and he rubbed her shoulders before pointing to the bench that faced the water. "Sit down, please, will you?"

She hesitated a fraction, wondering where he was going with this then lowered herself to the bench. The moon offered enough visibility that she was able to see his face. He'd shocked the tears from her throat with his high-handed, albeit gentle, maneuvering. She had to admit, he hadn't physically hurt her once. She could have pulled away and left had she chosen to do so…and she knew he wouldn't have stopped her.

He demanded, "Now, talk to me, please?"

She bit her lip; looked away. The urge to run away threatened to overpower her. The desire to share with Joseph the hurt in her heart took precedence. "You know as well as I do the kind of woman you want to marry. Only you didn't share those expectations with me until we were already…until it was too…"

Oh, Lord, give me the words. "My mother and my father were cops, you know that. I just never told you—in detail— what a lousy marriage they had," she said through gritted teeth. "I made the decision not to get involved with a cop…and then you came along and I thought maybe it would be okay. But—" she blew out a breath "—I now know that I can't live the life of what it would entail."

"I haven't asked you to marry me, Catelyn."

She flinched at the reminder. "True, but you were going to two years ago, weren't you?"

This time he jerked. "Yeah, I was."

She felt the tears trying to surface again and only stopped

them through sheer willpower. "You want me to be like your mother, stay home, do nothing but care for a family, have babies, all that. And like you said not too long ago, 'what's wrong with that?' And the answer is—nothing. There's absolutely nothing wrong with that—if that's what a woman wants to do." She lifted her hands, palms up. "I don't."

He rubbed his chin and looked at the ground, a flush covering his cheeks. "And you think I would expect that of you?"

"Yes!" He averted his gaze and she knew she'd hit a bull's-eye. But she wanted him to understand completely why they were wrong for each other. "Oh, maybe not at first, but eventually you would because, in your heart, that's what you want. You would drop little hints in the beginning, then those hints would turn to suggestions, then to outright demands. And when I didn't comply, not only would I feel guilty for not following my husband's requests, you'd resort to begging, guilt trips, whatever."

"You think you have me figured out pretty good, don't you?"

Catelyn could see his face, but couldn't read his expression. She thought she saw some anger, maybe—pity? But he didn't deny her accusations, either. Instead, he squatted in front of her. "Is that what your parents' marriage was like?"

She snapped her mouth shut, but it gave a betraying tremble. Instead of being angry with her, taking offense at her blunt, possibly overreactive words, he was trying to understand, offering her compassion, empathy.

The dam broke and the tears dripped one after the other down her cheeks. His hand lifted to wipe them away, but there was no stopping the flood.

Catelyn blurted, "Yes, and it was awful." Her voice squeaked, but she didn't care. "They loved each other in the beginning, had such high hopes and dreams. They had me."

She tapped her chest then let her hand drop. "And they just pushed it all away, like it wasn't important. They shoved me to the wayside. The job became everything and they started competing with each other. Who could earn the most decorations, make the most collars, be the best cop." She whispered, "Hurt the other one the most."

"Aw, Catie. Why didn't you ever tell me all this?"

"I…just couldn't. It makes me so mad, so hurt, I try not to think about it."

"So that's why you needed space and…" His quiet words struck her heart. She'd hurt him, too, two years ago.

"And when you left like you did—" she broke off, bit her lip "—I'm sorry, Joseph. I've got to go." *Before I say anything else.* She stood and he rose from his crouched position, grimacing as his knees popped.

A small watery chuckle escaped her, breaking the tension a bit. "You're getting to be an old man, Santino."

"We don't have to be your parents, Catelyn." He lifted a hand and stroked her cheek, not letting her sidetrack him with a poor attempt at humor. "I care too much about you to let you sweep this under the rug. I think what happened two years ago goes a lot deeper than what you've touched on here."

She drew in another deep breath. "I need to leave, Joseph."

He followed her back to her car without another word. She could tell he wanted to push it. To get all the answers out of her. But right now, all she wanted was to go home, crawl into bed and pull the covers up over her head for at least a week.

But she couldn't. She still had a missing girl to find—and if Joseph's instincts were on target, there was still a murderer wandering free.

She definitely had her work cut out for her.

Emotions and feelings would have to wait.

Joseph let her go.

She almost wondered if she'd really blown it this time. Had she pushed him away for good?

Sighing, exhaustion cramped her and she pushed the emotion aside. She just couldn't deal with it anymore.

Pulling into her driveway, she noticed things had changed a bit since she'd left a few hours earlier. Crime-scene tape still covered the area, but the house stood in darkness. She'd forgotten to leave a light on.

Memory of the earlier incident spooked her and she shivered as she put the car in park and turned it off. She really wished she'd left some kind of light burning. Or that she'd asked Joseph to follow her home.

Get a grip. You're a cop.

True, but sometimes criminals returned to the scene of the crime, she had no backup with her—and she'd never liked coming home to an empty, dark house. She had enough of that when her parents had worked the same shift late into the night during her early teenage years before her father...

Unclipping the strap from her Glock 23, she decided she'd rather be safe than sorry.

Inserting the key, she unlocked the door.

At least it was locked this time.

Slowly, she inched it open and stepped inside. And just stood there.

Listening.

Two minutes passed. Three.

Nothing moved. Not a whisper of a sound that shouldn't be there.

Breathing a little easier, she flipped on the foyer light, walked into her den and winced. Quickly, she gave her house a walk-through.

All clear.

Back in the den.

What a mess. "Great. Just what I want to deal with tonight. Lord," she said aloud, "I don't know how this case is going to turn out, but help me remember You're still in charge. And I don't know where all this is going with Joseph, why I felt so compelled to spill my guts like that, but…"

Cutting off her prayer, she waded through the mess to pick up a picture knocked facedown on the mantel. She turned it over and felt tears well up again.

Her parents on their wedding day.

Never had two people looked so happy. Her dad in his uniform dress blues and her mother in a gown of white. Big grins and bigger dreams.

Oh, God, why? What happened? Where did it go wrong? Why couldn't they work it out? Compromise? Something? How did they turn into enemies? These two people who were supposed to have each other's back?

She studied her dad's face and a fury like she'd never known herself capable of filled her. She screamed aloud at the photo, "How could you leave me like that? How?"

Frisbee style, she flung the picture across the room where it whacked the wall and fell to the floor, broken glass littering the hardwood.

Just like her heart.

A thousand tiny pieces. Shattered, never to be put back together. *Why didn't You do something, God? Why? With all Your power and all Your love, how could You just let them…*

With shock, she stopped her anguished prayer and dropped to the couch. What was she saying? Was she blaming God for the downward spiral of her parents' marriage and the twists her life had taken as a result?

Breath whooshed from her lungs as she considered that.

Maybe she did blame God.

But she loved God.

And God had failed her. At least that's how she felt.

Tears coursed down her cheeks as she got up, still pondering this self-realization she'd stumbled onto. Mindless, she began to clean the mess left by her intruder. Zombie-like, she walked into the kitchen for a trash bag, then back to the den to throw away broken pieces of one lamp and other odds and ends she'd had sitting on her mantel.

Mad at God.

He'd failed her.

He'd left her when she needed Him.

Just like her father.

Just like Joseph.

Which brought her back to why she could never be with Joseph. She couldn't live up to his expectations for one, and she didn't know if she could get past her fear of what marrying another officer would entail.

Numb, she moved to the entertainment center. The large wooden structure had been jerked away from the wall so the thieves could unplug the DVD player and other electronic equipment she'd had.

For a moment, she studied the television. The great gaping hole in the center of the screen stared back her, a one-eyed monster. It definitely looked like it had been smashed on purpose. The TV was an older model. Maybe they were mad that it wouldn't bring much money and had decided to take the anger out on the object.

Whatever. She almost didn't care. She'd been battered one too many times tonight, emotionally and physically.

Grasping the edge of the large piece of furniture she pulled it back. As she stepped for another tug, she felt something soft under her foot. Bending down, she picked it up.

A baseball cap.

With the logo from the deaf school on it.

With two fingers, she carried it into the kitchen. Grabbing a brown paper bag from under her sink, she placed the hat in it and folded the top of the bag closed. A chill slithered down her spine. Was this break-in related to the case? If so did that mean she and Joseph had someone worried? Was someone after her? She set her jaw with determination. Well, no amount of danger would scare her off. A girl was missing and Catelyn was determined to find her. Alive.

Time to see who the hat belonged to. Hopefully, the perp left a few strands of hair with the roots intact. Catelyn gave a tight smile.

DNA was a wonderful thing.

And maybe if she tried real hard, focusing on the case would keep her from focusing on herself—or Joseph's truthful words.

After Catelyn left, Joseph drew in a deep breath and shoved his hands in his pockets. His heart hurt for her, this woman that he still loved. He was surprised the admission came so easy to him.

But he did. Loved her still. Even after she'd broken his heart. The hurt had been so acute, he'd run. To a new job, a new state, a new life.

And still, not for a lack of trying, he'd never forgotten her or successfully moved on. Simply put, he'd missed her.

Turning, he walked up the steps to the front porch and settled himself on the swing. The clear night allowed him a good view of the Big Dipper, the Little Dipper, a glimpse of the Milky Way and the rest of the scattered twinkling stars. God's tapestry.

What do You see, God? Up there from the other side? Where do we go from here? Personally and professionally? Kelly's still out there, Lord and I know there's a team searching even as I sit here. I pray You're keeping her safe. Keep Catie close, let her know You're there for her. So much to pray about, God. I'm glad You know my heart. Show me how to reach her, how to help her face her past and her fears.

Joseph's thoughts and prayers turned to Dylan. During the questioning, Joseph had carefully observed the boy. He'd not shown any signs of lying. Yes, he'd been scared, worried, anxious. But not guilty.

Although he'd been deceitful in not telling the full story the first time he'd been questioned, Joseph could see why he'd felt he could leave out his being at the school. If he was telling the truth, and Tracy was alive at the time he'd left the area, then, in his eyes, he wouldn't have anything of relevance to add. Of course, he should have come clean, but Joseph could understand why he hadn't.

If his story was the real deal.

Tomorrow, he and Catelyn would spend their day investigating the case. Another Saturday spent working. But at least he'd be with Catelyn. Maybe she'd open up more with him tomorrow during the course of the day.

He had a feeling she'd left a lot unsaid tonight.

The door opened and his dad stepped out. "Joseph? Are you all right?"

"Fine, Dad. Just sitting here...contemplating, praying a little. When are Ethan and Marianna coming home?"

"They'll be back tomorrow. Said they had some news for us."

His interest piqued, he quirked a brow at his parent. "Really? What kind of news?"

"Not sure. Ethan's been thinking about transferring into South Carolina Law Enforcement Division, so they may be moving to Columbia."

"Ouch. What does Mom say to that?"

"She's not happy about it, but wants what's best for all."

"Yeah." His thoughts returned to Catelyn.

"Catelyn's gotten ahold of you again, huh?"

Startled at his dad's astute assessment, Joseph let out a low laugh. "Now what would make you say that?"

"We're a visual family, Joey," his dad said, pulling his childhood nickname from the past. "I see a lot. And you didn't take off two years ago for New York because your life was going along smoothly."

"But I never said…"

"You didn't have to, son. Some things a dad just knows."

"Huh."

"So, she's gotten ahold of you again."

"Yeah, she has." Why bother to deny it? "But she's got this…anger deep inside her about something. It's like a silent fury that's bubbling underneath the surface ready to erupt. I think it has something to do with her father's death, but I'm not sure. I just get that idea from reading between the lines. I think she's got a lot of anger towards God, too. And until she gets that resolved, she and I really can't go forward."

"Wow. That's a lot to deal with."

"For her and me. Because I want to be there for her when it happens. I think it's going to have to in order for her to be able to move on with her life. I just wish she'd share it all with me."

"Are you up to it?"

He met his dad's eyes. "I have to be. I think if we can get through whatever's going on inside her right now, we can deal with whatever the future throws at us. I think."

"All right, well I'll be praying, too. She's a lot different from your mom, but she's a good woman. A man could consider himself blessed with a girl like that. Night, son."

Speechless, Joseph watched his father reenter the house. Then he raised his eyes back toward the heavens and in suspicious wonder, said, "Huh."

His phone rang.

Catelyn.

He listened as she kept her tone professional and distant. "I'm on the way to see the graveyard shift at the lab. I found a baseball cap behind my entertainment center. I'm going to see if someone is willing to process it tonight to see if we can get anything useful from it. We've got to find Kelly, Joseph. I really feel like her time is running out."

EIGHT

Sluggishly, Catelyn pulled her weary body from her bed. A late-night run to the third-shift crime lab to drop off the hat had her arriving back home for the third time that day and climbing in bed around two in the morning.

She'd allowed herself five and half hours of sleep before rising and dressing for the day ahead. Anticipation and dread churned within her at the thought of seeing Joseph again. He had told her to call him if she got anything, but the lab had been crazy and she'd finally left without getting the information she wanted to grab a few hours of sleep. Hopefully today she and Joseph would learn something new.

Joseph.

Now that she had time to contemplate her revelations to him last night, she felt almost embarrassed, wondering if he'd think less of her for revealing some of her innermost feelings.

Her mind said he wouldn't, not the Joseph she'd known two years ago, but her heart still wondered. Gulping down a bagel and some coffee, she headed toward the office. She didn't bother to call Joseph, knowing full well he'd probably be there when she arrived.

Sure enough, when she pulled into the parking lot, his car sat in the spot nearest the door. Butterflies tickled her insides.

As much as she wished it wasn't so, she realized she really looked forward to seeing Joseph.

In spite of her embarrassment over last night's outburst.

Entering the building, she strode to the elevator and rode up to the third floor. Stepping out when the double doors opened, she ran smack into a hard chest made harder by a Kevlar vest. "Oomph."

Masculine hands grasped her upper arms and set her back. "In a hurry, Clark? If I'd known you were that anxious to throw yourself into my arms, I would've done something before now."

"Back off, Johnson," anther male voice demanded.

Tim Johnson's brows shot Heavenward and he obeyed Joseph's order, holding his hands in the universal sign for surrender. "I was just kidding. Catelyn and I are old friends."

Catelyn stared in surprise at the danger glinting in Joseph's dark eyes. Catelyn shot lasers at Joseph and he stared for a moment before shrugging. "Right."

He turned and walked back to his desk. Catelyn gave Tim a disgusted look and trotted off after Joseph. He sat at his desk, not bothering to look up when she approached. "You think that was necessary? That I can't take care of myself?"

Finally, his eyes lifted to meet hers. Innocence radiated from him. "What?"

She opened her mouth to reply then snapped it shut. "Forget it. We've got a girl to find."

"I agree."

Her phone buzzed and she grabbed it. "Hello?"

"Hey. This is Sandy."

Crime-lab Sandy. "What's up?"

"I've got that DNA from the hat."

"What? Already? When I left last night, the place was a zoo."

"You're a friend who was victimized. I stayed late."

Touched, Catelyn responded. "Wow. Thanks so much."

"If you can get me a sample from whoever you think it belongs to, I can try to match it up for you."

"That'll be what I'm working on today. What color was the hair?"

"You're looking for a redheaded male. Good luck."

"Yeah, and thanks again," she said.

She hung up.

Great.

"What do you have?" Joseph asked from his spot behind his desk.

Nothing about last night. Good. Breathing a sigh of relief, she said, "Sandy extracted the DNA, but we need something to match it up to."

"You've got a picture of the hat?"

"Yes."

"We can show it around, but it could belong to anyone. However, just giving an educated guess, I'm willing to bet that it belongs to someone between the ages of fourteen and eighteen."

"Redheaded and male, too."

He quirked a brow. "That helps."

"I know. At least it's a start. And if we come across a red-headed teen, we can ask for his DNA."

"Let's start with Billy Franklin again. There was just something about that kid when we talked to him at school. He was nervous, scared. And he has reddish-blonde hair. Let's catch him at home."

"Sounds good to me."

On the way to the Franklin residence, Catelyn called to check on Zachary only to be told there was no change in his condition. She told the nurse, "Please call me as soon as he wakes up."

"If he wakes up, I will," came the sympathetic response.
"Right."

Catelyn relayed her conversation to Joseph, who sighed then said, "I have another question for Billy. Not only do I want to know who the hat belongs to, I want to know if he knows who Zachary hangs out with and who he could have been with the day before his sister's funeral."

Ten minutes later, they pulled into the Franklin's driveway. Catelyn had called and let Mrs. Franklin know they were coming. Fortunately, they'd been home and were free to meet. Billy was on his way home from his coach's house where he'd been hanging out with some friends of his from the baseball team.

Joseph knocked on the door then stepped back, his badge in his hand. Less than a minute later, Mrs. Franklin opened the door. "Hello."

"Thanks for agreeing to meet with us."

"Anything to find Kelly."

The forty-something woman opened the screen door and stood back to allow Catelyn and Joseph to step inside. Then she led the way to a small family room where she gestured for them to have a seat.

Running a hand through her mussed gray hair, she said, "Billy's on his way. I called his cell a few minutes ago and he promised to be here soon."

"That's fine," Joseph said. The woman looked worn out. "I know this is an incredibly difficult time for your family, but I promise we're doing everything possible to track down your daughter."

She gave a small sad smile. "I know. It just seems like there should be something more that I could be doing. Some way to help find her."

"Unfortunately, there's not. You're staying by the phone, keeping your cell phone charged in case she sends you a text message. That's about all you can do." He didn't bother to tell her they'd already tried to trace Kelly's cell phone and hadn't had any luck.

The door slammed and Billy entered the den. He'd lost weight. His hands shook as he nodded at the two officers sitting in his den. Joseph frowned. The poor kid was falling apart. "Hi, Billy."

"Hi." He slouched onto the couch, shoulders hunched, his head pulled low, like he was trying to impersonate a turtle.

"Sorry to pull you away from your friends."

"It's all right. I wasn't having much fun anyway. Alonso was there, though. You should…" He stopped and looked away.

"I should what?"

"Nothing."

"You've got a big game coming up in a few days, don't you? Play-offs?"

"Right." No enthusiasm whatsoever. Depression? Possibly.

Joseph pulled the picture of the hat out of his pocket. "Do you recognize this hat?"

Billy leaned forward and took the proffered photo. He studied it for all of three seconds before he said, "Sure. Practically every kid at the deaf school has one. Kelly even has one. They give them away the first day of school in a kind of welcome-back-to-school package."

Catelyn pulled in a deep breath. Joseph flicked a glance in her direction. Great. "Do you know anyone it could possibly belong to?" The break-in happened last night. Plus the hat probably belonged to a deaf kid.

"No, I don't know."

"All right, one last question." The real reason for their visit. "Do you know who Zachary was hanging out with the day before his sister's funeral? His mother didn't know and no one can tell us."

Billy's body language went from slouched and lethargic to ramrod straight and tense. His eyes slid to his mother then back to Joseph, before ending their journey on the floor. "I don't know. I saw him right before the visitation, but he never said anything about being with anyone. He just seemed mad."

"Mad? Not sad?"

The boy jerked. "No, he wasn't sad. He didn't like his sister that much."

Well, that sort of went along with what Dylan had told them. Catelyn shifted, but didn't stop writing on the pad in front of her. Joseph probed deeper. "Why do you say that?"

"She was mean. And always causing trouble for Zachary."

"Do you think Zachary killed his sister?"

"No. As much as she got on his nerves, he wouldn't kill her."

"Why not?"

Billy shrugged, glanced at his watch and shifted. "I don't know, I just don't think he would have. I mean he didn't like her, but she was still his sister, you know?"

"The first day we started this investigation, a young boy by the name of Chad thought Dylan killed Tracy. What do you think?"

"Chad was in love with Tracy. He'd never have hurt her. He was obsessed with her or something. But Tracy thought he was a loser and wouldn't have anything to do with him. Dylan and Tracy used to be friends until he started dating Kelly. For some reason Tracy didn't like that, but I don't know why. She never said anything. I do know Zachary wanted Kelly for himself, but Kelly was a good girl." His throat bobbed again. "She wouldn't have anything to do with Zachary." This time his eyes met Joseph's. "I wouldn't let her."

"Because of his gang affiliations?"

"Yeah, mostly."

"What do you know about the gang, The Skulls?"

Fear bleached his face white. "I already told you. I stay away from them. I don't want to have anything to do with them."

"But they've infiltrated the deaf school. They've got deaf kids joining this gang. Do you think they've done something to Kelly?"

Tears flooded his eyes and he sighed, glanced at his watch one more time. "I don't know." He stood. "Look, I wish I could help, but I can't."

"You keep looking at your watch. Do you have somewhere you need to be?"

"I told Coach I'd be right back. We're discussing baseball strategy for the game on Tuesday night."

Joseph looked at Catelyn. "Do you have any more questions you need to ask?"

"Just one, if I gave you a description of a redheaded deaf teen, who would be the first one to come to mind?"

Confusion flashed across his face along with a smidge of irritation. "I don't know. Um, Lee Myers, maybe."

Joseph stood, facing the teen. "All right, thanks. If you think of anything else, give us a call, will you?"

"Right." Billy looked at his mother. "Gotta go, Ma. Coach is feeding us supper. Cooking out. I'll be home around nine, okay?"

Anxiety written on her features, Mrs. Franklin nodded. "Fine. I'll tell your father."

"Thanks." He leaned over and kissed her cheek. Waving to Joseph and Catelyn, he slipped out the door.

After thanking the woman for her time, they headed at a fast clip for the car.

"What's your hurry?" Catelyn asked.

"That kid is up to something. I want to follow him and find out what."

* * *

Catelyn hurried around to her side of the car and hopped in. Joseph climbed behind the wheel and pulled from the curb. Billy's taillights flashed for a brief moment at the stop sign at the end of his street. He turned left and Joseph followed a safe distance behind.

"That kid is royally scared of something," Catelyn muttered as they pulled out of the subdivision onto Pine Street. Cars whizzed by, but Joseph had no trouble keeping Billy's vehicle in sight.

"Yeah, I get the same feeling. I just want to know what it is."

"Or who it is."

"Right."

Catelyn rubbed her eyes, turned to him and said, "He saw us there and didn't ask any questions about Kelly."

"You noticed that, too?"

"Right off. Most people worried about someone see us and immediately ask if there are any new developments."

"True, but he is a seventeen year-old kid."

"Granted. However, he just sat there. He also shows symptoms of depression. Although, I guess those could be attributed to whatever he's afraid of, too."

He wheeled around the next corner and entered a very prestigious subdivision. "Hey, isn't this where Coach Dillard lives?"

"Sure is. And there's his house."

"Well, it's exactly where Billy said he was going."

Joseph pulled up to the curb. They had a pretty good view of the huge backyard from their vantage point.

"Look, they're signing."

"And there's your brother."

Joseph frowned. "He didn't say anything about a baseball get-together today."

"I guess he doesn't feel like he has to report in to big brother about his activities." She gave him a smile.

"Guess not."

"Who's that?" Catelyn pointed to another young man. One she recognized as the kid who attacked Dylan at Joseph's house. "That's Chad, right?"

"It sure is."

"And look, there's a redheaded kid signing to Alonso."

They exchanged a look then Joseph shook his head. "Naw, it couldn't be that easy."

"Of course not. And we don't have any reason to ask him for his DNA."

"I see several of those hats on heads over there."

"The deaf school and the high school have really come together to give these kids a great opportunity. A lot of good deaf baseball players at the deaf school, but no team. A high school that needed good players. Couldn't ask for a better combination."

"Not to mention a winning one. That coach, Alan Dillard, sure is committed to his boys, isn't he?"

"It's good to see. Kids need role models like that."

Billy came out of the house and Coach Dillard immediately walked up to the boy and put his arm around his shoulders. Billy kept his eyes on the wooden flooring of the deck.

The coach leaned over and said something in Billy's ear. Billy shook his head, shoving his hands into the pockets of his baggy jeans. Coach Dillard nodded, slapped him on the back and then stepped up onto the large wooden deck. He clapped his hands, waved his arms and motioned for the boys to gather around.

Coach Dillard started to talk and sign at the same time and Joseph turned to Catelyn. "I've seen enough." They started forward and Catelyn grabbed his arm and pointed. Billy had turned from the crowd and isolated himself in a far corner.

"The kid's hurting…or something. Something more than his sister being missing is going on with him," she murmured.

"I agree." Joseph sighed and shoved a hand through his hair. "All right, I'm going to talk to Alonso about that hat. I also want to ask Coach Dillard to let me know if one of his players is missing a hat that he normally wears. Feel free to eavesdrop if you can see what we're saying. You coming?"

"Absolutely." Catelyn followed behind him, approaching the house from the front. Stacy Dillard answered the door and soon she led them through the house, to the sliding-glass doors and out onto the wooden deck. Alonso immediately spotted Joseph, surprise and curiosity drawing him toward his brother.

Joseph waved to the coach, who frowned and walked over. "Something I can help you with?"

"Just need to ask my brother a few questions."

The man's brows rose. "Can't this wait?"

"If it could I wouldn't be here."

Coach Dillard shrugged and backed off. "No problem, then." Joseph pulled Alonso aside and the two talked for a moment. Catelyn decided to take advantage of the time and crossed to catch Coach Dillard before he could get into another conversation. She had a few questions of her own.

Joseph signed, "Sorry to intrude, but I wanted to ask you a couple of questions."

Irritation darkened the young man's eyes, but he didn't protest, just nodded. "What do you want to know?"

Joseph pulled the photo of the hat from his pocket. "I'm seeing these things everywhere. Now, I know where they came from, I just need you to tell me if one of the guys here lost one between last night and today."

Alonso shrugged. "Not that I know of. I can keep my eyes open, though."

"It would be a redheaded kid who wears one all the time. The hat is worn and practically falling apart. My guess is, the kid wears it every day. I wanted to ask you because you're on both campuses."

Blowing out a breath, Alonso thought for a moment. "Either Ron Camp or Tyler Hathaway. They both go to the deaf school."

"Do you know where they live?"

"Ron lives across the street from the school in that neighborhood, but I don't know which house. Tyler lives in Gaffney. He's a day student and buses in every day."

"Does he play baseball?"

"No, neither of them is on the team. And I'm glad because I don't like them much."

"Why not?"

"I think they're involved in that gang. The one Tracy was with. From what I hear, they're always causing problems in school, but haven't done anything to get themselves kicked out, yet."

Interest definitely perked, Joseph made a note to visit these two young men as soon as possible. "Thanks, Alonso. You've been a big help."

Alonso left and Joseph turned to find Catelyn heading his way. "Ready?"

"Yep."

"You disappeared on me. Did you learn anything?"

"Not much. Coach Dillard said he'd keep an eye out for one of his guys who lost a hat, but said some of these kids wear a different hat every day."

"He's right about that. All right. I guess that's it for here. I've got two guys we need to track down. Redheaded deaf kids that wear the hat with the school logo on a regular basis."

"Let's go then."

Twenty minutes later they arrived at Ron Camp's house.

Joseph climbed from the car and looked around. "Doesn't look like anyone's home."

"Should have gotten the number and called."

"No, I don't want to scare these guys off. I they're somehow involved, they could pull a major disappearing act."

"True."

Joseph walked up the path to the front door and rapped his knuckles on the wood.

No luck.

Catelyn's cell phone rang and she lifted it to her ear. Joseph watched her listen then her eyes shot to his as she said, "Thanks, Sandy."

"What docs she have?"

"She said she managed to pull off some writing that had almost completely faded from the edge of the hat."

"What was it?"

"The initials, *T.H.*"

Joseph gave a little smile. "Well, well. Let's head to Gaffney and pay Mr. Tyler Hathaway a little visit."

NINE

Tyler Hathaway proved to be an elusive young man. No one answered the phone at the residence. "That doesn't mean he's not there." But he wasn't. Joseph sent a text message to Alonso. "Quick question. Where does Tyler Hathaway hang out?"

Alonso's response came back immediately. "At the arcade on Stead street. Likes the free meals next door. That church on Stead Street. If he's not at home, you can count on him being there—if he could get a ride in. At least that's where they were hanging two weeks ago."

"Thanks." He looked at Catelyn. "Want to head over there?"

"Absolutely—" she looked at her watch "—but if he's not there, I'm going to have to leave pretty soon."

"Got something to do this afternoon?"

"An appointment. It'll just take me about a couple of hours. Then I can meet back up with you."

"Okay." He was quiet for a moment as they climbed into the car and took off. Catelyn thought he might ask her what she needed to do. He didn't.

She volunteered, "My mother. I need to go see her. I need to take her something she asked for before I walked in on my intruder."

She felt him grasp her hand and looked over at him. Comassion flared brightly in his eyes. "I'm sorry." He squeezed er fingers.

Catelyn shrugged. "I deal with it."

"Will you let me go with you?"

She hadn't expected that one. "Why?"

"Because I want to. I want to be there for you if you need 1e."

"But…" What did she say to that? "Are you sure?" The nought of having someone to lean on, to care about her, to care bout the effect visiting her mother had on her emotionally was lmost overpowering. Something she desperately wanted.

But did she dare trust him? With her life, yes. Her heart? Not there yet.

Visions of her childhood brought sheer anxiety shooting hrough her. "I don't know, Joseph. It's not exactly the most pleasant thing to do."

He tugged her hand and she leaned in closer.

"I want to," he insisted.

What if she let him close again and he decided she wasn't what he needed, what he wanted—again?

But what about what she wanted? Needed?

He let her go, concentrating on the drive. "It's a simple hing, Catelyn. Why are you having such a hard time letting ne back into your life when you know it's what we both want?"

Catelyn reeled away from him. "But I don't, Joseph. I don't know that that's what I want." But it was and yet… "And why are you pushing so hard when you've made it clear that I'm not wife material?" His flinch singed her heart, but she had to make him understand. "I just—" She broke off and pointed. 'Isn't that Tyler Hathaway?"

Joseph blinked, pressed the brake and followed her pointing finger. "That's him."

"You got the paperwork we need to arrest him?"

"Got it right here on the computer."

"Excellent. Let's go get the twerp and see what he has t say for himself." He gave her a hard look. "But don't think thi conversation's over. It's not."

Catelyn ignored him and kept her eyes on the young ma standing outside the arcade next door to the church smokin a cigarette.

Joseph pulled up next to the curb and they got out. Thei activity caught the young thug's attention and he straightened eyes narrowing.

"He's going to run."

No sooner had the words left her lips than Tyler threw hi cigarette to the pavement and took off, legs churning as fast a he could push them.

Joseph and Catelyn were right behind him.

Down the sidewalk they went, dodging the occasional pe destrian. Catelyn could feel Joseph right on her heels.

The kid was fast.

Fortunately, she ran three miles almost every morning. Sh knew she had the endurance to outlast him—as long as sh didn't lose him.

He darted around the corner of the next building an Catelyn felt a surge of satisfaction. She raced after him wit Joseph breathing down her neck.

Around the corner, down the next alleyway, she heard hi running steps skid to a stop. The clank of a chain-link fence.

Soon she had him in her sights.

He was clawing his way over the fence.

Without slowing down, Catelyn pounded up to him, graspe the back of his belt with both hands and pulled.

Tyler gave a harsh yell, but didn't let go.

Two seconds later, Joseph added his strength to the situation and within the blink of an eye, had Tyler on the ground, his hands cuffed behind his back.

Catelyn placed her hands on her knees and drew in a deep breath. Joseph was a little winded himself but that didn't stop him from patting the kid down and pulling out a knife and a pair of brass knuckles. "Nice assortment here," he grunted as he hauled the kid to his feet.

Catelyn shook her head to dispel the images of a previous arrest where she'd been stabbed. Nausea churned. She covered it up by signing, "If you'll promise not to fight, Special Agent Santino here will move your cuffs to the front so you can communicate."

Fury emanated from Tyler. He wasn't happy being caught. Too bad. She wasn't too happy with *him*. Catelyn continued. "Looks like you need a little time to calm down. Your interpreter will meet us at the jail."

Joseph jerked him to the car while Catelyn signed his rights to him. They'd have the interpreter do it again, just so no one could come back and say anything about her not being certified in sign language.

Tyler understood her. His glare never lessened. She told Joseph, "Better keep those cuffs in the back."

"I think you're right. We'll get him to the station and in the interrogation room and see how tough he is there."

The teen never once made an attempt to communicate on the way to the jail. Catelyn figured he was doing his best to figure out how to get out of this mess. He also didn't put up a fight once inside and they were able to remove his cuffs so that he would be able to talk should he choose to do so.

The interpreter was waiting when they arrived.

Once in the room, Catelyn sat across from Tyler, the interpreter next to her. Joseph sat at the end of the table. She stared at Tyler, trying to decide the best way to approach questioning him.

She glanced at Joseph. "You want to start?"

"Sure, you got the video set up?"

"Taping as we speak."

Catelyn informed him once more of his rights and he signed the paper saying that he understood them. She told him that he was being taped and then Joseph said, "You want to tell me what you were doing in Detective Clark's house, who was with you and where her stuff is?"

Joseph watched the kid jerk like he'd been punched on the chin. A new emotion crossed his face.

Anxiety.

Good.

"I don't know what you're talking about," Tyler signed.

Joseph leaned in, making sure the kid still had the interpreter in his line of sight. "Sure you do. You broke into Detective Clark's house, trashed it and stole a lot of her electronics. We know you were there. We have a warrant for your DNA and as soon as it comes back, we'll match it to the hat you left behind."

Tyler's eyes rounded slightly.

"Yeah, Tyler," Catelyn pushed, "you know, the one with the deaf school logo on it that has your initials on the inside edge?"

The teen shifted, his left eye began to twitch and he ran a hand through his greasy red hair. "Where's my lawyer?"

Joseph gave a mental groan. Up to this point, the kid hadn't said a word about wanting a lawyer although they'd offered. Catelyn looked at Joseph and sighed. "I'll let them know he wants legal representation."

Another long night loomed ahead. Joseph watched Catelyn leave, then turned back to the kid. And just stared at him.

Tyler refused to meet his eyes.

So Joseph just waited.

Finally the boy signed, "What?"

Joseph shrugged.

The interpreter glanced between them but kept quiet. She was a veteran interpreter and professional all the way.

Tyler stood abruptly. The officer standing just outside the glass door watched intently. He placed his hand on his gun. Joseph tensed, but signaled the man that he had the situation in hand. The officer relaxed, however he kept his hand near his weapon.

Joseph caught Tyler's eye. "Problem?"

"Do I have to wait for my lawyer?"

"I would if I were you."

Licking his lips, Tyler paced from one end of the room to the other. Joseph let him. He could handle the teen if he decided to turn violent.

The clock ticked. Tyler turned. "Do I get some kind of deal if I help you?"

Excitement leaped within Joseph. Finally, they were getting somewhere. He kept his expression neutral and signed, "Possibly."

Catelyn chose that moment to return, a portly, balding gentleman with a keen glint to his eye, in tow. She gestured to him and said, "Meet Edward Hale. Defense attorney for Mr. Tyler Hathaway."

After handshakes all around, they got right to it. Mr. Hale advised his client not to say a word, but the client had other ideas.

"I changed my mind, I don't want a lawyer. I want a deal."

Joseph rubbed his hands together and leaned closer, pushing a piece of paper in front of the kid. "Sign here and tell us what you know."

TEN

Catelyn decided to leave Joseph to the questioning. As soon as he was finished, she knew he'd call her. She had to get to the nursing home. Her mother expected her to be on time.

Actually, her mother seemed to be slipping more and more into her own little world and Catelyn wondered if she'd even notice her daughter was running about thirty minutes late.

Bounding up the steps and through the automatic sliding doors, she waved to the nurse behind the desk. "Hi, Thea."

"Hi, Catelyn."

"Sorry I'm late. I'm working a case that doesn't seem to have stopping points."

A sympathetic smile flashed across Thea's face. "I understand. She's awake and seems to be having a good day today. Much better than yesterday."

"Great, thanks." She hurried down the hall to the second room on the left and slowly opened the door. "Mom?"

"Catelyn, is that you?"

A good day. Her mother remembered she was coming, was waiting on her. Catelyn slipped into the room and blinked at the sight of her mother. Always she seemed to age a little more between each visit. In no way did she resemble the vibrant young woman pictured in the wedding photo that Catelyn had thrown across her den. White hair had obliterated the shining blond strands that used hang in carefully groomed waves. Her clear blue eyes had the look of confusion more often than not now.

But not today. Today Marilyn Clark's gaze landed on Catelyn with a shrewdness Catelyn hadn't seen in weeks.

"Sorry I'm late," Catelyn said as she entered the room.

"Big case?" The fact that Catelyn now worked as member of the same force her mother had served on was a huge source of pride for the woman.

"Yes." She changed the subject. "Here. I brought you something."

Her mother took the album from Catelyn and studied it. "I haven't seen this in years."

"Thea said you asked for it."

"I did?"

"Must have."

Her mom opened the book and looked at the first few pictures. Without raising her head, she said, "We had some good times, didn't we?"

Catelyn sighed. "Some." She shifted, uneasiness twisting within her. "You look like you're feeling good today."

Setting the album to the side, her mom said, "I'd feel better if you'd tell me what you're working on."

So Catelyn did, falling into the routine of acting like everything was fine and that the past hadn't happened, that her parents hadn't destroyed each other with Catelyn suffering the effects of their selfishness. Instead, she pretended, played the dutiful daughter, didn't vent, didn't ask why they hadn't loved her more than…

Pulling in a deep breath, she finished her account of the case. By this time, two hours had passed and Catelyn itched to leave.

Then her mother did something she hadn't done since she'd been in the nursing home. She reached over and clasped Catelyn's hand. Startled, Catelyn looked at her mother. The woman had never been big on affection and hadn't reached out for a voluntary touch in years. "Mom?"

"I'm sorry."

Heart thudding, Catelyn started at her mother. "What?"

Tears built in those aging blue eyes, and her mom looked away, giving a small sniff. "I'm sorry."

Perplexed, Catelyn stepped around to gaze at this woman she'd called mother all her life, but didn't really know. "For what?" She figured she was treading on thin ice, but had to know what her mother was sorry for.

"For what we did to you," came the quietest whisper.

Pain shafted through her. Why now? What had incited her to bring this up now?

"It's—" she couldn't say it was all right because it wasn't, but "—it's in the past, Mom. Just…forget it."

"I can't. I know I will soon as a result of this horrid disease, but while I'm thinking clearly…" She pulled Catelyn closer. "I'm sorry. Will you ever find it in your heart to be able to forgive us?"

Lightning zapping her wouldn't have shocked her more. What did she say?

Say, I forgive you, she told herself.

Say it.

Her throat worked, her lips moved, but she couldn't vocalize the words. Too much hurt rested within her. Instead, she pushed the words through her tight throat and whispered, "Did you know what Daddy was going to do that night? Did you know he was going to put that gun in his mouth and pull the trigger?"

Her mother flinched, her chin wobbled. "No. I promise, I didn't know."

A whimper escaped Catelyn, but she leaned down and placed her forehead against her mother's. Anger, hurt and resentment battled within her, but the need to feel her mother's arms around her won out over her need to express her rage at this helpless woman. "I want to forgive you. Hug me," she pleaded. "Just…love me."

Slowly, thin, wiry arms lifted and wound around Catelyn's stronger, youthful form.

And for the first time that she could remember in a very long time, her mother hugged her.

Catelyn sobbed on her shoulder and thought she heard the words "I do love you."

Joseph stepped back from the room. Catelyn wouldn't appreciate it if she knew he'd followed her here.

He'd walked down to the room to find Catelyn in her mother's arms, sobbing out enough tears to fill Lake Bowen. Heart aching for her, wanting to be a part of the solution to her problem, he turned to go back to the waiting area.

"Joseph?"

Uh-oh. Caught.

He did a one-eighty back to face the door. She stood in the doorway wiping her eyes, looking about fourteen years old.

"Hey, sorry. Look, I didn't mean to interrupt…"

"What are you doing here?"

"I decided to come over after we finished up with Mr. Hathaway. Plus, I got the text message information from Zachary's phone for the day of the funeral. Thought you might want to see it. And, we need to track down Billy again."

She sniffed. "You have really rotten timing, you know that?"

"But a great sense of direction."

A chuckle escaped her. She wasn't mad at him. Relaxing a fraction, he opened his arms. "Need a hug?"

More tears flooded her eyes at the question, but she shook her head. "No. I need to get back to work. We need to go over those text messages."

"You can take a few minutes."

She sucked in a deep breath. "What else did you learn after I left?"

"Quite a bit, actually. I called to check on Zachary again, too. He's still in a coma, although the doctors are more enthusiastic about his waking up sometime in the near future. I told them to call us as soon as he starts to stir."

"Excellent."

"I've still got a guard on his door just in case the person who shot him decides to finish the job. He says the kid has some regular visitors like Coach Dillard and some of the other players, but it's been quiet with no problems."

"Good." Another deep breath and she was fairly composed.

He wished she'd taken him up on his offer of a hug. "Hungry?"

She nodded. "Starving. Have we stopped to eat today?"

"I don't remember."

She gave another laugh. "Then I'd say it's time."

"Let's grab something while we wait on a search warrant for the Hathaway residence."

"Tyler gave you enough for that?"

"Yep. Just waiting on the call."

They hurried out to their cars, Catelyn following behind Joseph back into town. They decided on a pizza place that served buffet style.

Joseph settled into the booth opposite her and admired the way she could be tough and delicate all at the same time. Strong on the streets, yet ate her pizza with all the grace of a lady. He smiled. His dad was right. Catelyn was different from his mother, but a man would be blessed to be loved by her. He cleared his throat.

"Did you have a good visit with your mother?"

She paused, pizza hanging in the air in front of her mouth. Then she deliberately took a bite and chewed.

Joseph just waited.

She swallowed and looked him in the eye. "It was interesting."

"Emotional?"

"To say the least."

"Are you going to share it with me?"

His phone rang, interrupting her answer. He winced, but snatched it up. "Hello?"

Catelyn swallowed the last of her water and watched Joseph give her the thumbs-up. He hung up. "We've got our search warrant and a team's on the way to the house. They'll meet us there with a copy of Zachary's text messaging log for the last week. We can see if any number stands out."

She tossed some bills on the table. "Let's go."

Joseph added his money and they took off out the door.

Catelyn watched the scenery whiz by.

Soon, they pulled in behind a black-and-white cruiser. Joseph stepped out. "Anyone home?"

The uniformed officer shook his head. "Not that we can see. No one's answering the door, anyway."

Joseph and Catelyn approached the house. Catelyn said, "Knock it in."

"What's going on?"

They turned at the sound of the voice coming from the street. A gentleman in his early fifties stood at the curb, two officers blocking his approach. Catelyn strode over to him. "Who are you, sir?"

"I'm David Hathaway. This is my house."

"We've been trying to get in touch with you. We have your son in custody and have a search warrant for this property."

Outrage turned the man's face a scary shade of purple. He exploded. "What do you mean you have my son in custody! Why wasn't I contacted? Where is he and no, you can't search this property!"

The two officers placed their hands on their weapons. Catelyn held up a soothing hand. "Sir, if you'll just calm down…"

"I will not calm down. What is the meaning of this?"

Catelyn explained the situation, adding the fact that his son's DNA had been found on the hat left in her house and they had tried to call to inform him but hadn't been able to reach him. Then she asked, "Will you please open the door?"

By the end of her explanation, the man's face had gone through several different shades of red to wind up a pasty white.

Without another word, he approached the house and opened the door. Stepping back, he waved them in.

Joseph asked, "Do you have any idea where Tyler might hide any stolen goods?"

"No, of course not. When can I see my son?"

"You're welcome to go down to the jail anytime."

A shout from the garage pulled Catelyn and Joseph in that direction. An officer led them through the garage into the backyard and over to a shed sitting on the corner of the property.

"Crammed full, Detective."

Catelyn stuck her head in and gasped. "Wow."

Tyler's father had followed. "What in the world? Where did all this come from?"

Joseph looked at him. "I take it you don't ever come out here?"

The man never took his eyes from the goods in the shed. He slowly shook his head. "Never. Once I started working so many hours, I hired a yard service that comes once a week. They have their own supplies. Tyler has some pretty bad allergies so I never asked him to do anything outside." He took in the scene again. "I can't believe this."

Joseph sighed. "What you want to bet this is related to all of the break-ins we've been having over on the west side of town?"

"I do believe you could be right," Catelyn agreed.

"All right, I'll call the guys in charge of that case and we'll let them come take a look."

"Hey, Joseph, look over there. A flip-flop and a backpack. Looks kind of out of place in all of those stolen goods. I sure would like to know who those belong to."

"Definitely."

Two hours later, they had matched up the flip-flop with the one found at the crime scene. It belonged to Kelly Franklin. Surprisingly enough, the backpack was Billy's, Kelly's brother. Once again, they had the third-shift crime-scene guys working overtime.

Joseph turned to Catelyn. "I think we need to find Billy and see what he has to say about his backpack being in that storage shed."

Catelyn stifled a yawn. "Sounds good to me." She glanced at her watch and groaned. 9:00. It was going to be another late night.

Joseph was eyeing her like he wanted to say something else. Not up to a big discussion, she slid around him and out the door, calling over her shoulder. "Come on, let's get going."

"Catelyn…"

"Yeah?"

He shook his head. "Nothing. Let's go find Billy."

Catelyn crawled into the passenger seat of the car and let

Joseph drive. She leaned her head against the back of the seat and sighed. *Please, Lord, let us find Kelly before it's too late.*

"Hey, you okay?"

"Yeah, just tired."

"We'll find her."

She gave him a weary smile. "I sure hope so."

He cranked the car and pulled away from the curb to head for the Franklin house. They'd called ahead, but had gotten no answer. Which was really strange considering the family was desperate for news about Kelly.

Joseph let the car idle in front of the dark, empty-looking house. "Huh. Wonder where they could be?"

"Do you have cell numbers for the parents?"

"Yeah." He pulled the mounted laptop around in front of him and typed a few keys. As he rattled off the first number, Catelyn punched it into her phone and waited. She looked at Joseph. "Voice mail."

He frowned and gave her the next cell phone number. "That's the dad's number. Bryan."

"Got it." She waited again. "Voice mail."

"I'm not getting a good feeling about this."

"Do you have any next-of-kin numbers?"

"I can find out. Hold on." He tapped a few more keys on the keyboard and gave her another number. "It's Kelly's aunt, her mom's sister. She lives on the west side of town. Libby Darlington."

Catelyn dialed it and perked up when someone answered. She pressed speaker so Joseph could listen in. "Hello? Mrs. Darlington? This is Detective Catelyn Clark with the Spartanburg Sheriff's Department. I need to…"

The woman interrupted. "Have you found Kelly?"

"No ma'am, we haven't. I'm sorry, but I need to ask you if you know where Mr. and Mrs. Franklin are."

"They're at the hospital. We think Bryan had a heart attack."

Catelyn gasped. "Oh, no. I'm sorry to hear that. I'll call if I have any news on Kelly. Thank you so much."

She hung up.

Joseph raised a brow. "To the hospital?"

"Yeah."

ELEVEN

The first person Joseph spotted when entered the waiting room was Alan Dillard. The man saw him and Catelyn coming toward him and rose from his seat to greet them.

After handshakes all around, Joseph asked, "How's Mr. Franklin doing?"

"We're still waiting to hear."

"Is Billy here? We need to talk to him."

"No, I haven't seen him. He's really the one I came down to support. Mrs. Franklin called me and asked if Billy could stay with me while they were here at the hospital. I came to pick him up, but…" The man shrugged. "I haven't seen him. Which is really strange."

Catelyn and Joseph shared a look. "Well, if you hear from him, will you give us a call?"

"Absolutely."

Joseph handed his card to the man then turned to Catelyn. "Why don't we go check on Zachary while we're here?"

Coach Dillard spoke up. "You can check on him, but I just came from there. There's been no change. Stacy, my wife, is up there, too, with Zachary's family."

Joseph thought for a moment. "I guess we'll see if we can track down Billy."

"I've already been calling all his buddies and no one's seen him. I hope he hasn't snapped."

"What do you mean?" Catelyn asked.

"I've seen some symptoms of depression. I've tried talking his parents into letting him talk to a counselor, but they're not having any part of it. They're consumed with finding Kelly. And now this…" He lifted his hands, palms up then dropped them to his side. "I don't know. I have to say, I'm worried, though."

Joseph shook the man's hand again. "Thanks for your help. If we find him, we'll let you know."

Alan nodded and returned to his seat.

Joseph turned to go and caught sight of two familiar figures walking arm in arm toward the exit located just ahead. They'd come from a different part of the hospital that shared the exit with the heart center. It was his sister and her husband.

"Marianna? Ethan?" he called.

Ethan turned, pulling Joseph's sister to a stop. He spotted Joseph and nudged the woman, signing Joseph's name with a crooked pinky twisted next to his right eye. She whirled, her long black hair fanning out behind her. Excitement lit her face and she ran to throw herself into her brother's arms. Joseph gave her a gentle squeeze. He pulled back to sign, "You've gained some weight, little sister."

Marianna whacked him on the arm. "Thanks a bunch." Then she smiled. "It's so good to see you. What are doing here? Is everything all right?"

Joseph held up a hand. "Whoa, whoa. Yes, everything's fine. Just a case we're working on."

Ethan approached with an outstretched hand. Joseph shook it while Catelyn hugged Marianna. Ethan said, "Good to see you. We just got back from our mini vacation and haven't had a chance to let everyone know."

"What are you doing here?" Catelyn asked, signing so

Marianna could easily follow the conversation rather than have to try to read lips.

Marianna and Ethan exchanged a look. Ethan cleared his throat and shrugged. "Just paying someone a visit. Nothing major. Anyway, we're headed over to see your parents. We both head back to work tomorrow." His gaze sharpened as he zeroed in on Catelyn. "Anything I need to know about?"

She snorted. "Captain has work waiting for you, don't worry. And I'll fill you in when I can, but right now, we really need to get going. We've got a missing girl to find."

Marianna frowned. "When can we get together?"

Joseph rubbed her back with one hand, signing with the other. "After this case is finished, I promise, we'll all go out for some fun. Maybe dinner and a movie, okay?"

Marianna, used to Joseph's and Ethan's workaholic ways simply rolled her eyes and linked her arm back through her husband's. With her right hand she signed, "Come on, you're not going back to work until you have to. And that's an order."

Ethan looked torn, but finally succumbed to the soulful, dark brown eyes peering up him. He shrugged. "Catch you later."

Joseph and Catelyn said their goodbyes and left the hospital to climb back into the car. Two hours later, Joseph slapped the wheel.

"It's almost midnight. He's not at any of his friends' houses. Where could he be?"

"I don't know." She rubbed a hand across weary features. "He's got that big game coming up. Surely he wouldn't do anything to jeopardize the team's chances for winning the tournament."

Joseph shrugged, thinking she might be right, then said, "If he is depressed, he might not be thinking clearly."

"True."

"Okay, so I'm going to call in a BOLO for Billy and then

I'm going to take you back to your car. There's really nothing more we can do tonight."

"Right, let's grab a few hours of sleep and meet back in the morning."

He drove in the direction of the station. Pulling a water bottle from the cup holder, he uncapped it and asked, "Are we going to finish our conversation?"

"What do you mean?"

"At the restaurant before we were interrupted. You were telling me about your parents."

Catelyn drew in a deep breath and Joseph held his. Had he stepped over the line in asking? He took another swig of the water as he waited to see what she would say.

"My father killed himself when I was seventeen."

Joseph choked, spewing the small sip of water he'd just taken. Catelyn didn't look in his direction, just stared out the window. He said, "I never knew that. I just thought it was an accident with his gun."

"That's what everyone believed. But the official report was he ate his gun. I've hated him ever since. I think I've had a lot of suppressed anger, too." She spoke in a calm, deliberate way, almost as though talking about someone else. "But now that I've figured that out, I'm going to be able to deal with it. I'm going to *have* to deal with it."

"Catie…" he whispered.

"Don't." She held up a hand. "I don't want your sympathy right now. I'll start blubbering."

"You never told me."

"I…couldn't. Until today. Because of my mother." She shook her head. "Amazing."

The numbness faded leaving a gaping wound in her heart. She felt the tears surface again. "Anyway, after he…died…my mother…she, um, she just…she kind of withered away. Quit the force, quit life, quit…me."

He reached across to take her hand. "I don't know what to say."

Catelyn pulled away. "There's nothing you can say. Your home became my haven. My escape. If your family hadn't treated me as one of your own, I don't know where I'd be today." She gave a short laugh. "The only reason I never tried alcohol or took anyone up on those many offers of drugs was because of your parents. I…didn't want to blow a good thing. I knew if I got caught up in that kind of stuff, your parents wouldn't let me back in their home."

"That's not true. They loved you and would've helped you, would have still treated you like one of their own kids and gotten you any help you might have needed."

She gave a small laugh and brushed at nonexistent lint on her khakis. Then she nodded. "You're probably right." Her eyes finally lifted to his. "I do believe you're right."

"See, God was looking out for you after all…in spite of the parents you were born to."

Tears flooded her eyes again and she sniffed, desperate to turn them off, but not quite succeeding. He changed the subject and she gave a grateful sigh.

"But why become a cop?" He turned into the parking lot and pulled the unmarked cruiser to a stop beside her car. "Why this profession when it seems to be the reason your parents messed up so completely."

This time the laughter that escaped her had a harsh ring to it. "Because I thought it would help me understand. I thought if I *became* them, if I walked in their shoes, I could somehow find some answers."

"And have you?"

She shrugged. Had she? With a start, she realized that those few moments with her mother today had gone a long way toward dispelling the raging fury she'd carried in her heart for so long. More so than working as an officer had. "I don't know. I don't know if I'll ever know."

"I want to be there for you, Catie."

"And I want you to be there, but I don't think I'm capable of having a relationship with another cop." She stared into his eyes and took a deep breath. "No matter how much my heart might want to."

With that, she climbed out of his vehicle and into her own, not bothering to look back. Because if she looked back, she knew he'd be watching her and she'd cave in to the urge to run into his arms, eating her words and throwing caution to the wind.

And with visions of the screaming matches she'd grown up with flashing in her mind, she knew she just couldn't do that.

Arriving home, Catelyn pulled into her garage this time and went in the back door. A quick inspection told her no one had been in the house during her absence except for the professional cleaning service she'd called in to repair what the vandals had destroyed.

Her house looked good, finally back in order—if missing a few electronics. She'd get an insurance check for that soon enough. No time to watch TV anyway.

She kicked off her shoes and looked longingly toward her bedroom. Fatigue gripped her, numbing her mind, pulling on her body. The day had been an eternity what with the visit with her mother, telling Joseph about her father, avoiding her feelings for Joseph and trying to stay on top of this case.

Now, she just wanted to sleep for a few hours before starting all over again.

But first she checked all the doors and windows one more time. Just to be sure.

Not usually nervous about turning the lights out, she realized she didn't want to be in the dark tonight.

Leaving the hall light burning, she crawled into her bed and prayed. *Lord, You've shown me some pretty incredible things about myself lately. I'm not sure what to think about everything, to be honest. Especially this thing that seems to be between Joseph and myself. I guess I'm going to have to leave that for You to figure out. And as for today with my mother—thanks. I needed that. I still don't understand why my father did what he did, I don't know why You couldn't have just…*

She cut off the prayer feeling the anger rise back up in her. It would take time, she figured. Time to process it all again. Maybe she'd never be at peace about it. The thought terrified her because more than anything, she wanted peace.

Peace, Lord. Please give me peace…

She must have drifted off because something awakened her. She lay still, wondering what it could have been. Usually once she fell asleep, she slept until her alarm went off.

Something had disturbed that. The air in her room seemed different. A smell that she didn't recognize. A combination of body odor and cigarettes?

Then she realized…

…someone was in here with her.

Her nerves bunched. Frozen, her eyes probed the shadows. Very little moonlight made its way through her heavy curtains. Usually she liked to sleep in pure darkness. The light from the hallway was out. Now the night seemed to press in on her.

Her heart pounding, her palms slick, she pondered what to do. How to react. Which way to move. Where was he? Not daring to move to alert whoever was in the room that she was awake, she calculated how long it would take to roll to her left, grab open the night stand and palm her gun.

The shadows shifted.

He was beside her bed.

She tensed her muscles to roll to the right.

Without warning, something soft fell across her face and pressure from above kept it there.

She was too late!

Flinging her arms up, she tried to push the object away. Felt hard fists clenched into the fabric.

She couldn't scream, couldn't breathe!

Someone was trying to kill her by smothering her with her own pillow. She kicked, bucked, turned her head and managed a small gasp of air before the small opening closed.

God, help me!

Churning her arms, she tried to punch. Her feeble blows fell on a bare arm. Panicking, she dug her fingernails in.

The arm flinched away from her and she managed to push the pillow to the side while her attacker fought to maneuver it back into place.

Another gasp of life-giving air. Then the pillow returned heavier than before. Brain racing, she frantically brought both hands up and felt a head, ears. She pushed, but couldn't budge the person above her.

Help! Help me! Her mind screamed; terror nearly scrambled her thinking.

Then an idea filtered through the fog of fear.

Fisting her hands, she laid her arms spread eagle on the bed then brought them up with all her strength, effectively boxing her attacker's ears.

A howl of rage and pain reached her as he flung himself back. As he jerked away from her, she grasped the mask covering his face. The sliver of moonlight caught on a lantern-shaped chin. Then he was in the dark and disappearing fast.

Kicking at the covers, Catelyn rolled to her right and landed on the opposite side of the bed. Fleeing feet headed for her bedroom door.

"Oh…no…you…don't!" she ground out through gasps for air and gritted teeth.

But she was on the wrong side of the bed. Her gun was in the other nightstand. Flipping herself over the bed, she grabbed the drawer and yanked.

Gun in one hand, cordless phone in the other, she took off after the escaping thug. She could hear him pounding through her kitchen, then the slam of the back door.

She punched in 911 and headed out after her target.

TWELVE

Joseph lifted his head from the kitchen table, rubbed the sleep from his eyes and looked around. He'd fallen asleep over the case files.

What time was it?

The stove clock read 1:38.

Time to get comfortable and get some sleep. He still had his gun strapped to his arm and his phone on his belt. His gaze dropped to the picture of the missing girl. Kelly Franklin. Was she still alive? Was she hurt? Suffering? Or was she already long dead, Tracy's killer striking twice. But she'd been alive after Tracy had died. That much he thought he knew. The flip-flop left at the first scene indicated she was at least still alive when she was taken from the campus.

And the other found in a storage shed full of stolen goods. Was she a part of the ring? Or had she stumbled on all of this accidentally? Digging into her life had shown her to be a "good girl" who hung out with the right crowd with the exception of Tracy Merritt. Kelly went to church every Sunday. Was friends with Alonso, girlfriend to Dylan, who had a bit of a shady past, but seemed to be trying to turn it around. Maybe Kelly was a positive influence on him.

Why was she at the school that night? To meet Dylan as he'd

said? But neither were dorm students. Because she lived in town, normally, Tracy wouldn't stay on campus overnight, but because she played basketball, she was allowed to be a temporary residential student.

So, Kelly and Dylan had planned to meet that night at the school for whatever reason. Kelly arrived early and got into an argument with Tracy. Dylan came upon them fighting, got into the thick of it, then left when Kelly wanted to finish whatever she and Tracy were arguing about.

He pulled out the text message log from the phones. Kelly and Dylan had arranged their rendezvous. Nothing about meeting Tracy. So it hadn't been prearranged. Tracy's cell had no texts that evening.

Zachary's had several to his coach about meeting for practice, confirming game times, baseball chit-chat, and then telling him about Tracy's funeral. Nothing unusual. Nothing revealing. Nothing to indicate who he was meeting with the day of the funeral. He could have received a text anytime during the day and met up with the person several hours later.

However, there was one text that Zachary had received about an hour before he was reported to have left the house. It read "Stay out of stuff that's not your business or you'll be very sorry."

The text came from Stacy Dillard's phone. This was a new twist. What was the woman doing sending that text to Zachary? Definitely something to ask her about tomorrow.

Joseph sighed and put the papers aside then reached up to rub his eyes.

And then there was Catelyn. What was he going to do about the only woman who'd ever driven him to distraction? Made him pace the floor at night thinking about how much he missed her and wished God would intervene to change her heart.

Her parents had done a number on her. Especially her father. Suicide…whoa. No wonder she was so angry.

Joseph sighed—and nearly jumped out of his skin when his phone buzzed.

Dispatch. What?

"Joseph here."

"This is Margo in dispatch. Sorry about the lateness of the call, but I just got a 911 call from your partner's house reporting an intruder. I know Catelyn pretty well and know you guys are working together. Figured you'd want to know."

"You figured right. I'm on my way. Thanks."

Joseph punched in Catelyn's number as his steps ate up the distance between the kitchen and the back door. Her phone rang four times then went to voice mail.

He hung up as he threw himself into his car. He could be at Catelyn's in approximately seven minutes. He planned to make it in five.

Where was he? Fury battled common sense. Her gun gripped in her right hand, she followed the path she thought her intruder had taken. Flashing lights pierced the darkness letting her know help had arrived.

But the guy she was after was getting away.

Had gotten away.

She'd lost him.

Winded, she leaned against the nearest telephone pole, and searched every nook and cranny within seeing distance.

He was around here somewhere, she felt sure, but with so many houses, bushes, trees, open garages, there was no way to figure out where he'd gone.

But they would search.

The squeal of tires caught her attention and she spun to see taillights disappear around the corner.

Picking up her cell, she dialed dispatch again. She needed Margo to patch her through to whoever was going to be in charge.

Eyes still scanning the shadows, she listened to it ring. Margo picked up before the first ring ended. "Catelyn, is that you?"

"It's me. He got away. I think he's heading north down Kendall Street. Get a car after him, will you?"

"You chased him?" She sounded outraged.

"I knew you were sending backup." Catelyn winced at the slight whine in her voice. "Anyway, I need some manpower out here to search the area and make sure he isn't taking refuge in someone's house or garage. I'm pretty sure he was in the car and is long gone by now, but we've got to check."

"It's on the way."

"Catelyn?"

She turned and her heart nosedived to her toes before banging back up. "Joseph? What are you doing here?"

"Margo called me."

"Ah. Well, she needn't have bothered. Sorry to get you out of bed."

"I haven't made it there yet. What happened?"

Remembered terror flooded her and she shivered. "I was asleep, or at least dozing. Something woke me up and I realized I wasn't alone in the room. Then I felt a pillow slam over my face…" She broke off and swallowed.

"Catie," he whispered, and wrapped his arms around her.

It felt like coming home.

The shakes set in and she felt the tremors rock through her. Yes, she was a cop, but she was still human. And she'd been personally attacked twice now. Her house and now her physical person. It was enough to throw the strongest person off her game.

She pulled in a deep breath and stepped back. "Thanks," she whispered without meeting his eyes.

"You're welcome. Are you okay? Did he hurt you?"

"I'm all right. I'm just wondering how he got in."

"Let's check it out."

Catelyn started back the way she'd come. She hadn't gone too far from her house when she'd lost the guy. Back in her driveway, she noticed something for the first time. "My garage door is open."

"You didn't open it?"

"No. I was stunned and mad when I came out chasing that guy and didn't stop to think about it, but I always close my garage at night. Maybe that's what woke me and not the smell."

"Did you lock the door going into the house?"

She sighed and rubbed her eyes. "I think so. I remember checking all the locks before going to bed, so yes, I'm pretty sure it was locked."

He stepped closer. "Let's see if we can get some prints off this. I can't tell by just looking at it, but I bet someone picked your lock. Did you notice if he was wearing gloves?"

She closed her eyes, forcing herself to remember what she'd felt when she'd reached up and felt his arm, his head, his fists. His ear.

"No, he wasn't and he was wearing two earrings in his left ear. Plus, I pulled a ski mask off and caught sight of his chin. Unfortunately, I couldn't see anything else.'

"So you wouldn't recognize him if you saw him again?"

"No," She sighed. "Probably not."

Two hours later, the crime-scene unit had finished up and the clock was pushing 3:45. There'd been no sign of her intruder. Joseph walked into her den and sat on the couch beside her. She had her knees pulled up, her forehead resting on them.

He reached over to rub her shoulder. "Are you going to be all right?"

"I don't know" came her mumbled response.

"It's a good thing you scratched him. The tissue they scraped from under your nails will be helpful—especially if it matches up with a guy who's got two earrings in his left ear."

"I know," she said to her knees.

Tilting her chin, he looked into her eyes. Eyes so blue, they usually reminded him of the ocean on a clear day. Only tonight, they were stormy gray. Vulnerability shone through the clouds and his heart clenched with sympathy.

He leaned closer, placing his lips on hers, feeling their softness, remembering their texture. He waited a moment, giving her the opportunity to pull away if she wanted.

Instead, a soft sigh escaped her and she let him kiss her. Just a soft, comforting kiss that touched his heart with tender fingers, yet left him longing for more.

Then he transferred the kiss to her forehead and she wrapped her arms around him to let him hold her.

Never had a moment been so sweet. He cherished it while he could, figuring when she got her feet back under her, she'd be off and running again.

"You'd better go," she mumbled against his chest.

"I know." He didn't move. She was letting him hold her, letting him see her vulnerable side and he didn't want the moment to end.

"You're not going to get much sleep," she warned him.

"I've gone on less."

With a sigh, she pulled away and his arms ached with loneliness. The sensation startled him, then he realized she was right. He should go.

He stood, and she gave him a small shove. "Give me a wake-up call, okay?"

"Sure. Try not worry. Your guy's probably not coming back."

"Probably not, but I'm still getting an alarm system put in."

"I can't believe you don't have one already."

She shrugged. "I've thought about it, of course, even had a company come out and give me an estimate. They're pretty expensive and with Mom in the nursing home…"

"Doesn't her pension pay for that?"

"No. She quit the force, remember?"

"So you…"

"Yeah, me." She waved him to the door. "Go on, get out of here. I'll see you tomorrow…um, today…in a couple of hours."

He lifted a hand and ran a finger down her cheek, started to say something, then closed his mouth and walked out the door.

THIRTEEN

Catelyn couldn't believe it. First, she'd let him kiss her after she'd given him a list of reasons a relationship between them would never work. And second, the big lug had slept in his car for the past—she looked at the clock—three and a half hours. She'd fallen into bed after setting her alarm and only rolled out fifteen minutes ago. She'd slept hard, her body craving the rest, and yet she'd been restless, too, worried her intruder might come back. And feeling guilty for resting when Kelly was still missing.

Joseph hadn't told her that he was planning on standing guard because he knew she wouldn't let him…or would, at the very least, lose sleep over his act of chivalry because she'd feel guilty that she was snug in her bed while he earned a crick in his neck.

The man knew her well for the most part.

Standing in her kitchen sipping a cup of the strongest coffee she could stand, she looked out her window and watched him stir.

He cared about her. She'd have to be comatose not to see it. The thought warmed her and scared her to death.

But she just couldn't get past her parents' lousy marriage—and the fear that she couldn't live up to Joseph's expectations of what being a wife entailed.

Although she realized she desperately wanted to. As long as she could be his wife and do her job. But that wasn't to be. He wanted a wife who'd be happy staying at home and there was no way that was going to be her.

That line of thought startled her. For so long, she'd refused to even consider marriage to another cop simply because of her childhood. But Joseph, ever since their first meeting when she'd been a hurting teen and he'd been the brother of her best friend, they'd had a connection…a…something.

So, did that mean if Joseph suddenly decided he would be happy having a cop for a wife, she'd change her stance on marriage to a police officer?

Groaning, she reached up to massage the back of her neck with her right hand, then finished of her coffee. She set the mug in the sink and looked back at the man in the car.

She did know one thing, though. No matter how conflicting her feelings, she cared for the guy. Maybe even loved him. Probably did. Okay, definitely did. Always had. Always would.

Pouring the rest of the ten-cup pot of caffeine into a thermos, she grabbed her lightweight police jacket and headed out the door and over to the car.

A light tap on the window roused him. He opened one eye and glared at her. She smiled and remembered the times he'd fallen asleep at his parents' home after a large family meal. His mom or dad would try to wake him and Catelyn, Marianna and Gina, two of his sisters, would watch and giggle about how grumpy he would be. Nothing had changed in all those years.

The window slid down. "Go away."

"You're an idiot," she said, hearing the affection in her voice.

"I know, but I couldn't just leave. I was…"

"Worried?"

"Huh. Maybe. I know you can take care of yourself pretty

well, but..." He shrugged and opened the other eye. "Is that coffee?"

She laughed at the pleading tone in his voice.

Opening the door, she settled in the passenger seat. "You drive and I'll pour."

"Deal." Cranking the car, he pulled away from the curb and rubbed the stubble on his chin. "Guess I'll clean up when we get to the station."

"What's the plan today?"

"I want to talk to Billy Franklin about his backpack and that flip-flop showing up in the storage shed."

She handed him the brew. "We probably should have pulled him out of bed last night and demanded some answers."

"I think we had enough to deal with last night. So, we grabbed a couple hours of sleep. We have to watch out for ourselves, too."

She rubbed her eyes. "I know you're right, it's just that Kelly's missing and we've still got a killer out there. It feels wrong to sleep even for a minute."

Joseph placed his coffee cup in the holder and reached over to squeeze her hand. "I know. We'll find her, though. Right now, I want to find Billy Franklin. I haven't been able to track him down all day."

She smiled at him, remembering his tender gentleness only a few hours earlier. Her dad never would have...

Her smile slipped and she said, "Have you called Coach Dillard?"

"Yeah. He said he hadn't heard from Billy and didn't have any idea where the kid might have gotten to. He did mention that Billy wouldn't miss the big game."

"How's his dad doing?"

"Better. It wasn't his heart. He had an anxiety attack."

"No wonder. I can't say I'm surprised."

Joseph reached for his coffee once more as he drove and Catelyn considered her feelings for the man. She wanted things to work out between them more than she'd thought possible.

Especially after last night…

But could she lay it all on the line like that? Trust him with her heart? Fully open herself up to someone else. A cop? One who wanted a traditional stay-at-home wife? Could she get past her own fears of what marrying another cop would entail?

She shuddered at the thought, but couldn't help the yearning desire to answer each question with a resounding yes. But the truth was, she just didn't know.

"Give me fifteen minutes, then we'll head over to the Dillard house. I want to talk to Stacy Dillard about that text message she sent Zachary."

She nodded. "She may be at church. Let me call and see if anyone is home."

He disappeared into the building and Catelyn got on the phone.

Mrs. Dillard let them in, albeit reluctantly. Joseph stepped through the door, taking in his surroundings—and the fading bruise on the woman's left cheekbone.

"What's this about, Detective? I have a sick child upstairs."

Joseph raised a brow. Were they going to do this in the foyer?

As if reading his mind, Stacy motioned for them to precede her into the den area. Catelyn sat on the edge of the nearest recliner. Joseph chose the love seat.

Stacy stood in the doorway, arms crossed. Joseph cleared his throat. "Mrs. Dillard, why don't you have a seat?"

She did.

Catelyn intervened. "I'm sorry Alan Jr. is sick. We won't take much of your time, but we need to ask you about Zachary."

"That's what you said on the phone."

"When we saw you at the funeral, you said you didn't understand why we thought Dylan would be a suspect in Kelly's disappearance. You thought we should be looking more at Zachary."

The woman took a deep breath and nodded. "Yes. Yes, I did say that."

"Then Zachary ends up shot and we find a text message on his phone from you."

Stacy paled, her right eye twitched. "I see."

Catelyn looked at Joseph. He nodded. He'd noticed she didn't ask which text message they were asking about.

"You threatened him."

She grimaced. "I wondered when that would come back to haunt me."

Joseph got up and wandered over to the glass gun rack. "That's a nice set of rifles you have there."

"They're my husband's." She twisted her fingers.

"Did you shoot Zachary?"

The woman let out a laugh. "What? You've got to be kidding. I was standing there in line with you when Zachary took off with you guys right behind him. When would I have been able to shoot him?" She waved a hand. "And I didn't want to shoot him anyway, I just wanted him to keep his mouth shut."

The woman had a point. She didn't shoot Zachary and she had two police officers who could give her an alibi. But did she know who shot him or did she hire someone to do it? He made a note to pull her financial records. "What was the text about?"

"Zachary knew Alan and I were having problems. I…met with a…friend. Zachary saw me meeting with…this friend. I was desperate—and stupid. I thought if I took a tough stance, Zachary would back off."

"Did he?"

"No, he wanted money to keep quiet."

"Blackmail?"

"Yes." She swallowed hard. "I asked him for some time to get the money together."

"So you were going to pay him?"

"Yes."

And that was as much as she was going to say, Joseph could tell. He wondered if her reticence to talk had anything to do with the bruise on her cheek. "I'm going to need the name of your…friend."

His phone rang. "Excuse me." He left Catclyn talking to Stacy while he took the call from one of the dispatchers. "Hello?"

"Billy Franklin was spotted at the church where he attends. The one on North Spring Street."

"Thanks."

Joseph hurried back into the den. "Come on, Catelyn. We've got to go pick up Billy." He turned to Stacy. "We're not done yet."

She shrugged. "I'm not going anywhere." Then she bit her lip. "Just don't tell Alan, please."

Joseph didn't make any promises, just followed Catelyn's brisk jog to the car.

FOURTEEN

Catelyn threw herself into the seat and slammed her door. "She didn't shoot Zachary."

"Nope. I think she's got some major marital problems, but I don't think she shot the kid to keep him quiet."

"What do all of these boys have in common?"

"They're all in high school. And they all play baseball."

"Right. That's what I've come up with. But there's something else tying them together, too. I just can't figure out what it is." She gritted her teeth as he took another turn. "Sandy said she'd put a rush on the DNA, to see if the evidence they got out from under my fingernails matches anything in the system."

"Okay, so what else? Somehow these guys with the baseball team are involved."

Joseph rounded a corner then took a sharp left.

Catelyn's breath whistled between her teeth as the scenery zipped past her window. "And Billy knows more than he's telling."

"You think someone's got his sister and is threatening to kill her if he tells what he knows?"

"It's possible, but what does Billy have that's of use to someone else? He's just a kid."

"He saw who did it and they're using Kelly to keep him quiet."

"But why not kill him, too? Kill both of them?"

"I don't know."

Catelyn's phone rang. "Hello?"

"Hey. This is Sandy."

"Sandy, do you ever sleep?"

"Not when I've got a case this big going on. The tests finally came back on that wood chip you found. It's the kind of wood that baseball bats are made of. It's ash wood and yes, ash is used for a lot of other things, but after studying that piece more, my guess is it came from a baseball bat."

"Was any blood or anything on it?"

"I found a piece of hair, no blood. Tracy never bled on the outside of her skull, just the inside. The hair matches up with Tracy's. I believe if you find a baseball bat with a missing chip, you'll find your murder weapon."

"You're worth your weight in gold, my friend. Thank you so much."

"Okay, now I'm going home to sleep for a few hours."

Catelyn saw they were getting close to the church. "You've more than earned it. If you hadn't stayed on top of things in the lab like you've done, we wouldn't be anywhere near solving this thing."

"This one kind of hits close to home. I'm friends with Dylan's mom, too."

"Thanks again, Sandy. Catch you later."

Catelyn hung up and relayed the information to Joseph. She finished up just as they pulled into the church parking lot.

Both hopped out of the car and entered the church. The service was over, people spilling from the auditorium.

Keeping her eyes open, she looked for any familiar faces milling around. Seeing none, she nodded for Joseph to take the opposite end of the lobby to watch those exiting the sanctuary.

She signed to him, "Do you see anyone?"

"No," he signed back.

She pulled back into the lobby and finally spotted a group of deaf kids signing near the exit.

Joseph caught her eye and followed her over to them. "Excuse me," she signed. "Would you guys mind talking to us outside?"

The boys stilled, eyes on the two cops who'd just interrupted their conversation. "This way, please, all of you."

Eyes darting back and forth to one another, they followed her outside where Joseph thanked them for their attention. Catelyn got down to business. "All right guys, have any of you seen Billy?"

"None of your business, Cop."

Catelyn honed in on the smart mouth. "Excuse me?"

"Bobby, shut up."

Joseph turned to the young black boy who'd just spoken. "And you are?"

"R.J., Ricky James, but I go by R.J. Yo, Coach and Billy left a while ago. Billy said he had to make a phone call and went to the lobby. Coach Dillard asked me what was up and I told him. He took after Billy like a streak of lightning."

Catelyn met Joseph's eyes. That didn't sound good. "Do you know where they went?"

"Nope. When Coach Dillard asked me where Billy went I told him and he said for us to catch a ride with one of the youth workers who would help get us home."

"Do you guys come to church every Sunday with Coach Dillard?"

The boy shrugged. "Most Sundays. Coach is real religious and likes us to come with him. He says we're his future and he's watching over his investment. Or something like that. We like Coach and think he's cool. Church is all right, too."

"All right. Thanks, R.J."

"I hope you can help Billy out. He's been real depressed lately what with his sister missing and all."

"You wouldn't happen to have any idea what happened that night she went missing would you?"

"No, man. I wish I did. I like Kelly, she's a good kid."

Joseph turned to the rest of the crew, signing and voicing at the same time. "Do any of you know where Coach Dillard and Billy might have gone?"

Bobby, Mr. Smartmouth, spoke up. "They had business and went to take care of it, obviously."

Catelyn lasered him with her eyes. "What kind of business? Gang business?"

A flush crept up into his cheeks. "Wouldn't you like to know?"

Joseph wanted to pop the kid in the mouth—or at least arrest him for something. Catelyn looked like she felt the same way. He ignored the kid and turned to the one who seemed willing to help. "R.J.?"

"That, I don't know. Coach Dillard just said he had to take care of something and it wouldn't wait."

"Where would they go to take care of this business? Someplace special?"

"Probably at his house. That's where he does everything. But I don't think Billy would go there. He's been mighty weird about Coach Dillard lately. Maybe at the high school? Coach's got an office there and spends a lot of time in it, studying teams, videos of different players and stuff."

Catelyn looked at Joseph. "You think?"

He shrugged. "I think that would be way too easy. But let's give it a shot. We just came from his house so I doubt he'd take his business there with his wife and kid."

"Right. Let's head for the school."

They thanked the boys and headed over to the high school.

* * *

The place looked deserted. Knocking on the door brought no response. Joseph peered in another window. "So do you think Tracy's death is related to the gang situation with Zachary wanting out or something else?"

"That's been in the back of my head ever since Dylan told us about it. But I'm thinking it's connected to something different. Tracy's death doesn't seem like a gang killing. She was cracked in the head with a blunt object—probably a baseball bat—and that sounds more like an impulse killing, spur of the moment, she made someone mad kind of thing."

"Yeah, that's what I think, too. The evidence isn't there for a gang killing."

"I sure wish Zachary would wake up so we could talk to him."

"I'm worried about the person who doesn't want him to wake up."

"That's why we've got a guard on him."

Fifteen minutes later, they pulled in the parking lot of Esterman High. Two cars sat in the parking lot. Joseph recognized the red Bronco from their visit to Coach Dillard's house. The blue Toyota looked familiar, too.

Joseph draped his wrists over the steering wheel, his brow creased in thought. "You know how we were brainstorming what all these guys had in common?"

"Yes."

"What about a coach?"

He nodded. "But why kill Tracy?"

"I have no idea. Let's go ask."

He blew out a breath and pulled his phone from the cup holder. "All right, let me call for backup, then let's see what we've got."

"Go for it."

He had the first six digits punched in when a shot rang out.

FIFTEEN

Weapons in hand, Joseph and Catelyn headed to the gymnasium where the shot had come from. Nerves bouncing with every step, she visualized various scenarios. Had the bullet found its target?

Catelyn got on her radio and called for an ambulance. "Shots fired."

"Backup's on the way," the dispatcher reassured her.

"Tell them to keep their sirens off. I don't want to alert anyone we're here yet."

"Ten-four."

Joseph found a window and looked in. Catelyn approached the door, and standing off to the side, reached over to turn the knob. It twisted easily beneath her palm.

The door swung inward.

She nodded to Joseph and, leading with his gun, stepped through the opening. Catelyn followed then moved ahead of Joseph.

Moving slowly, feeling Joseph at her back, she kept her ears trained for any warning sound. Her eyes took in every detail of the building. They'd come in the side door that opened directly into a hallway lined with closed doors on either side.

Catelyn tried the first one she came to.

Locked.

Joseph tried the next three.

All locked and no sound coming from behind them.

The door she and Joseph had entered just moments before cracked open. Catelyn swung her weapon around to train it on the opening. Joseph did the same.

Heart pounding, she waited. A gun came around the edge.

And Joseph stepped in front of her.

She snapped her gun so the muzzle pointed to the ceiling and stepped to the side so she could watch the door.

What was he doing?

She had to push aside the anger thrumming through her. She'd have to deal with that—and Joseph—later.

A uniformed officer slid inside followed by three more.

Catelyn released a whispered breath of relief. Joseph motioned for the officers to hang back. They nodded.

She shot Joseph a we'll-talk-later look and turned back, trying door knobs as she went.

Then she heard voices.

Catching Joseph's eye, she motioned him over.

Silently, he joined her.

"Where is she?!" Another shot and a bullet pierced the door. They both jumped.

Billy. Catelyn raised a brow and Joseph moved in, twisted the knob and pushed the door open, yelling, "Freeze! Police! Put the weapon down."

They stayed in a safe zone on opposite sides of the open door. Catelyn sneaked a look around the door frame.

Three pair of startled eyes focused in on the sudden intrusion. Billy held a gun in his right hand.

"Hands in the air, now!" Catelyn ordered.

"Billy," Joseph said, "put the gun on the floor."

The boy, tears streaking his face, shook his head. "No way. He knows where Kelly is but won't tell me. I'm out of time!"

"We're here now, Billy, just put the gun down so we can sit down and figure it all out."

"You'll just let him go, but you don't know what they've done."

"Then tell me. What has he done?"

Coach Dillard interrupted. "Nothing. Billy's distraught. He needs counseling."

"And you're going to need a doctor if you don't tell me where my sister is!" Spittle flew from his mouth as he screamed at his coach.

Joseph intervened. "Billy, come on. We can't settle anything if you have that gun."

"He'll kill me," he practically sobbed. "He killed Tracy and he's got Kelly."

"Who, Billy?"

"Him!" He waved the gun at Coach Dillard.

Catelyn watched a look of frustration pass over Alan's face. He held his hands up as though in surrender. "I don't know where he got this idea or why he's chosen me, but I can assure you, I had nothing to do with anything happening to the girls."

"Liar!" The gun waved wildly and Catelyn's heart clamped at the thought of shooting this kid.

"Billy, Billy," she soothed. "I promise, we'll work it out, just put the gun down."

She wondered if she was going to have to call in the hostage-negotiation team.

Joseph met her eyes. He was thinking the same thing.

"Here, look." Billy's hand reached for his pocket.

"Wait!" Joseph hollered. Billy froze.

"What are you going for?" Joseph asked a little more calmly.

"Pictures."

Catelyn saw Alan Dillard's body tense. She asked, "What kind of pictures, Billy?"

"Pictures of Kelly."

Joseph's mind raced. What if the kid was telling the truth? He'd noticed the subtle change in Dillard's posture. A sudden awareness that this situation might not go in his favor?

The tension, already thick, just tightened a bit more.

"Billy…" Coach Dillard started.

"Be quiet," Joseph ordered the man. He turned back to Billy. "Show me the pictures."

The kid reached into his pocket with his left hand and pulled out several snapshots. "He sent me these. I know he did."

"How do you know? Did you see him?"

Billy's brow creased even further. "No, but it had to be him. No one else knows what I do." He motioned with the gun for the coach to move back away from him. Then he walked forward and threw the pictures on the table just inside the door.

Unfortunately, he stepped right in front of Joseph, turning so the gun was pointed away from Alan for a brief second.

Alan took advantage of that and launched himself at Billy as the kid stepped back. The gun went flying, only to land inches from Billy's fingertips. He screamed and scrabbled for it.

Catelyn and Joseph reacted immediately. She went for the gun while Joseph went for Billy. Catelyn knocked the weapon from his grasping fingers.

Alan Dillard had him pinned on the floor. Several SWAT members swarmed the large office, guns pointed at everyone not wearing a badge.

Joseph pushed the man off Billy and hauled the youth to his feet. "Please, please, believe me. I promise you'll understand. Just look at the pictures."

Catelyn's skeptical look didn't escape Joseph's notice; however, she seemed to make a conscious decision to deliberately soften her stance and walked over to pick up the photographs.

A gasp escaped her as she studied the first one. He handed Billy over to one of the uniformed officers and crossed the room to look over her shoulder.

"Whoa."

"What's the date on that newspaper?"

"Yesterday."

Hope leaped within him as he studied the face of the terrified young girl glaring at the camera holding a newspaper. "She's still alive."

"Looks like it. But for how much longer?"

Joseph told Coach Dillard. "All right, fellas, let's head down to the station and see if we can hash all this out."

Alan narrowed his eyes. "Is that necessary? You saw who had the gun." He looked at Billy. "What happened, Billy? Why would you do this?"

Not giving Billy a chance to respond, Joseph said, "Yeah, it's necessary. I want to know why he thought he needed a gun to confront you and why he thinks you sent these pictures of his sister."

"Can we do this here? I'd prefer it if we could keep the media from getting ahold of this."

"Sorry, we'll expect you in our station within fifteen minutes." He didn't have any reason to arrest Alan—yet. But he still wanted to talk with him.

"Are you arresting Billy?" Alan demanded.

"Absolutely. You can't just go around waving a gun at people. But I also want to hear his story." He turned to one of the officers. His name tag read Bud Bridges. "Will you see Dillard gets to the station?"

"No problem."

"All right. You ready, Catelyn?"

She nodded, her eyes still on Billy, a frown creasing her forehead. Joseph asked, "What's wrong?"

"Nothing." She shook her head and rubbed her nose. "I... Nothing. Let's go."

They headed for the station, Joseph praying that they could finally resolve this case in the next few hours. His churning gut told him it probably wasn't going to be that easy.

Catelyn stomped into the interrogation room. She was starting to feel like she should move her bed into one of the rooms and change her address.

Billy fidgeted, crossing his arms in front of him then fiddling with the sleeve of his plaid shirt. He plucked a button from one cuff and it rolled to the floor. He didn't even blink.

Catelyn sat across from him and his parents who flanked him on either side. "Mr. Franklin, are you sure you're feeling up to this?"

The man nodded, weariness and despair oozing from him in almost visible waves. Catelyn took a deep breath and laid the pictures of Kelly out so they were visible for all to see. Mrs. Franklin sucked in a deep breath and studied her daughter. Then she said, "But this is good, right? It means she's still alive." Hope gleamed in her eyes.

She turned the tape recorder on, went through the list of introductory questions having him verify his name, birth date, etc. Once done, she said, "Start talking Billy. What happened? Where have you been?"

Tension had his body nearly vibrating. "I need to find Kelly. I've tried and tried, but I can't...I just...can't. I've run out of ideas and...time..."

"Who took her?"

"Coach Dillard did."

"You say that with absolute certainty. How do you know?"

Billy swallowed hard. "Because she called and told me she saw him kill Tracy. She didn't know I was just a minute away from the school. She begged me to help her then her phone got cut off."

"Why call you? Wouldn't she text message you? And don't say she did, we already checked her records."

"Normally she would have text messaged me—if she'd had time, but she sounded desperate and scared. She might be deaf, but she can still talk."

Catelyn murmured, "I did some checking on her. Her hearing loss is a lot like Marianna's." Joseph's sister couldn't hear much, but she had excellent speech.

Joseph nodded. "Okay. So she called you."

"Yeah. When Kelly didn't come home, I went looking for her. I figured she was probably meeting Dylan, so I went to the deaf school. They liked to meet there and hang out with the other kids before curfew."

"Did you see her?"

He sighed and rolled his eyes to the ceiling. "Yeah. When I got there, it was already dark. I saw Tracy lying on the ground –" his Adam's apple bobbed once "—dead, I think. Behind Tracy, I saw a man. He was arguing with Kelly. Kelly was hysterical, screaming that he'd killed Tracy. He was trying to get her shut up. He had her by her left wrist and she was trying to kick and hit…" He swallowed again. "He lifted the bat to hit Kelly and that's when I stepped out of the bushes and told him to put it down."

"Who was it, Billy?" Joseph pressed, leaning in to stare the kid in the eye.

"Coach Dillard. I told you, he killed Tracy and grabbed Kelly."

Catelyn jumped in. "Why haven't you told us this before now?"

He swallowed hard. "Because Coach said if I told anyone he'd kill her! I couldn't let him hurt Kelly." He swallowed again. "While Coach was dragging Kelly away, she signed, 'Coach and Tracy lovers.' And something about a secret room."

"Whoa." Joseph sat back. "Alan and Tracy were having an affair? What about this secret room? Did she say anything more about that? Where it was, who it belonged to? What was in it?"

Billy blinked at all the questions then said, "I guess they were having some kind of affair, I really don't know. And I don't know about a secret room, but that's what she signed. I wanted to go after her, but—" he rubbed his head "—I didn't dare. He was serious about killing Kelly."

"So, you just watched him put her in his car and drive away?"

"Yes." Shame flashed, then impatience stamped his face along with worry. "I thought I could find her! I thought I could…get her away from him and then go straight to the police, but he was too good, too smart for me, too… Look, you've got to find Kelly. He knows that I'm going to tell you all this and he's going to kill her!"

"Relax, Billy," Joseph said. "We've got him in a room down the hall. He can't get to her right now."

The boy sat back in his chair with a huff. He rubbed his arms and his sleeves slid up.

Catelyn reached out and grabbed his wrist. "What's this?"

Billy jerked away from her. "Nothing, I scratched myself."

She sat back with a thump. "Scratched yourself, my eye. That was you in my house! You tried to kill me?"

Billy leaped to his feet, fists clenched at his sides. "You're crazy."

Catelyn eyed Joseph who kept a watchful eye on things.

She planted herself in front of the boy. "You tried to kill me. Don't try to deny it. I pulled the mask off your face, you've got the scratches on your arm that are going to match up to the DNA in the system. Why don't you just come clean and tell us everything?"

Billy buried his face in his hands and let out a sigh. He seemed to wither into himself as he slumped back into his chair. "He told me I had to get rid of you. He said you were getting too close, interfering in everything." He looked up and had tears in his eyes. "I'm sorry, but he said he'd kill her if I didn't do it."

"Why didn't you just tell someone?"

"Because who would believe me?" He exploded. "Coach is like a god. Everyone in this town thinks he's the greatest thing in the world. And me?" He shrugged. "No one would believe me. Coach even laughed at me when I said I would tell. Then he said he'd send Kelly to my parents…bit by bit." His Adam's apple bobbed again. "I believed him. I couldn't take the chance. I…didn't want to hurt you…I didn't want any of this to happen…I just didn't know what else to do!"

Catelyn stood and paced, ignoring the boy's shocked parents. She looked at his ear. He'd removed his earrings. Billy's mother cried quietly. His father stared at the son who'd just confessed to attempted murder.

She whirled back. "Were you in on the break-in at my house that night? Stealing my stuff?"

"Yeah. I was there."

"And your backpack in the shed?"

He swallowed hard again. "I told Coach I'd had enough. I wanted him to let Kelly go and I promised I'd keep quiet, I'd keep Kelly quiet, too, but I couldn't keep doing what he wanted me to do." A tear leaked down his cheek. "He gave me the flip-flop. Said if I didn't obey him, the next thing of Kelly's that he gave me would be a finger. I had the backpack with me when we unloaded the stuff. I guess I left it there in the shed."

"Maybe hoping someone would find it? And force you into a confession?" Joseph questioned softly.

Billy shrugged. "I don't know. Maybe."

"All right." Joseph sat back and crossed his arms. "You'll have a hearing, and your parents can post bail for you—if you make bail. Attempted murder of a police officer is serious stuff."

Billy was already shaking his head before Joseph's last word. "No way. I want to stay here. I'll be safe here. Coach is going to be so mad. He knows I've squealed on him. If you let me go, he'll kill me." His lips tightened. "I just couldn't figure out why hadn't killed Kelly and me both yet. That's the thing. I kept thinking what's he waiting for? Why does he keep dragging it out? Then it hit me. He's waiting for the big game. He's waiting for me to win it." This was said without any cockiness whatsoever. The kid was a brilliant ball player and he knew it.

And he was probably right. Coach Dillard wanted to move up in his career—and felt he couldn't do it without Billy's help.

Leaving Billy in the hands of jail personnel, they made their way to the room where Dillard was supposed to be waiting. Catelyn looked in. "It's empty."

Joseph frowned. "Try the other one."

She marched to the next room and gave a disgusted grunt. "What is this?"

"What do you mean?"

"It's empty, too."

"Who was the officer we left him with?"

"I think his name is Bridges."

"Great." Joseph headed for the information desk. Catelyn followed.

He asked the officer behind the computer, "Could you page Officer Bridges, please? I need to speak with him."

The man nodded and picked up the phone. A minute later, he hung up. "He's not answering. Let me call him on his phone." He punched in a few more buttons and asked for the man. "No answer there, either. I don't understand. Let me just get into this program..." More typing on the computer. Then his brow shot up. He looked up from the screen. "He called for help about five minutes ago, declaring an officer down."

Catelyn nearly screeched. "What?"

SIXTEEN

Joseph and Catelyn bolted for the door and raced for the car.

He told her, "We need to find Dillard. If everything Billy is saying is true, he's going to go after Kelly. I should have told Bridges to cuff Alan."

"But we had no reason to place him under arrest," Catelyn protested as she yanked her car door open.

"Yeah, I know. Guess we do now." His jaw clenched, he slammed his door and cranked the vehicle.

Catelyn buckled her seat belt. "He knew he was busted as soon as Billy opened his mouth. Attacking and injuring an officer is the least of his problems if he's caught."

"I have a feeling we're seriously running out of time to find this girl alive." Wheeling out of the parking lot, he asked, "So, where to first? The coach's house or back to his office? Where would he go?"

"I'm going to get someone to cover all the bus stations, highway exits and the airport. There's no way he'd go back to his office or his house—would he?"

Joseph hesitated at the stop sign. "You wouldn't think, but if he's got Kelly at one of those locations, he's going to have to go there to get her." He grabbed his phone. "I'm going to get units covering both places immediately."

She nodded. "Sounds good."

He placed the calls then gripped the steering wheel. Finally he turned left.

Catelyn added, "But something else is bothering me."

"What?" He wondered if she was going to confront him about his actions in the gym earlier.

There went her teeth again, digging into her full bottom lip. He looked away. Now wasn't the time to notice how attractive she was. Instead, he focused on her words, which were about the case, not his faux pas—the one where he stepped in front of her. Relief flooded him. Maybe she was going to let it go.

He wasn't going to hold his breath on that one.

She said, "Those pictures of Kelly. They're really nagging at me."

"Okay, let's go over them."

Catelyn pinched the bridge of her nose and closed her eyes. "She's sitting in some, standing in others."

"And she's holding a newspaper in all of them, pointing to the date."

"What kind of room is she in? There's something about the room."

Joseph pictured the frightened teen and his gut clenched. They really needed to find her. "I couldn't really tell anything about it. It was a pretty close-up picture."

"Paneling." She snapped her fingers.

"What?"

"That's it, it's got to be. It's the paneling, the wall behind her."

He was confused. "That stuff is very commonplace. Nothing special about that."

"But it's the same as the paneling that was in Coach Dillard's office." Her eyes had the satisfied look of someone who'd just figured out a difficult puzzle.

"Well, if that's where they took the pictures, she wasn't there earlier when we came in on Billy threatening them with the gun."

"But what if they have her nearby? What if she's being held at the school somewhere?" Catelyn's excitement started to grow. Joseph could see it in her snapping blue eyes.

"How would that be possible?" Joseph played devil's advocate as he took a left turn to head for the school like she'd suggested instead of the coach's house. "There's a cleaning crew and people there practically around the clock. Someone would have seen or heard something."

"Just think about it. Alan Dillard's office is set apart from the main school building. It's on a back hall in the gym. All he has to do is put a sign on the door asking for maintenance not to enter his office. And remember, Billy said something about a secret room."

"Someone would get suspicious."

"Maybe not. Baseball season is intense right now. No one would question him spending a lot of time at the school or in his office after hours. So—" her words slowed "—tomorrow's the big game, right?"

"Right." He wondered where she was going with this line of thought. With Catelyn, he was never sure, but she usually made sense in the end. So he listened.

"Okay, so Coach Dillard is warning him against going to the cops. Why? He has to know inevitably, the kid is going to crack and say something."

"Like today."

"Exactly. So, he was hedging his bets and hoping Billy wouldn't say anything until after the game tomorrow."

The light came on for Joseph. "And that's why Billy was running out of time. As soon as the game is over, he and Kelly lose their value and are dead."

The school came into sight. "Right."

Catelyn blew out a sigh. "Well, his car's still here."

Joseph put the car in park. "Because you were right on it when you said he had unfinished business to take care of. Come on, we can't afford to wait on back up. Kelly's life is on the line."

Catelyn called and got a warrant on the way. She wanted to search that office. Every nook and cranny. And like Joseph said, there would be no waiting for backup. If Alan had Kelly, every second counted.

In what felt like a rerun of their actions just a few hours earlier, Joseph and Catelyn drew their guns and entered the building.

This time, though, they knew which door to aim for.

Once again, they took their positions on either side. "Police! Open up!"

Nothing.

Catelyn shot a look at Joseph who nodded. He stepped back, lifted a foot and kicked the door. It slammed in against the wall and bounced back. Joseph moved in, gun raised, using his body to block the door from banging shut.

The room was empty.

Catelyn walked over to the nearest wall and started tapping. "You got the door covered?"

"Yep."

Tap. Tap.

She worked her way around the room. Up one wall, down the next. Tap. Tap. Thud. Thud.

"Hello, what have we here?" She quirked a brow at Joseph. She was onto something.

Fingers explored the paneling and then her palm brushed up against a slight bulge in the wall.

She pushed it and the paneling separated, revealing a door as tall as she.

Catelyn swung the door open to expose a small living area with a door that must be a closet and a bathroom complete with a sink, shower and toilet.

"Joseph!"

He rushed up to stand beside her. A teenage girl lay on a twin-size bed, hands bound in front of her, but not moving.

"It's Kelly. I'll call an ambulance." He reached for his phone.

"I don't think we'll need that ambulance after all."

Catelyn swung her gaze up to see Alan Dillard, gun in hand, step out of the room she'd figured to be the closet.

SEVENTEEN

A mixture of fear and anger coursed through Joseph. Fear for Catelyn and anger at himself for not covering the closet.

Catelyn's nostrils flared, her gaze flitting between the man with the gun and the girl on the bed. "Well, well, came to finish up your dirty work, huh?" Disdain dripped from her voice.

"Shut up and drop your weapons."

Catelyn slowly lowered her piece to the floor, keeping her eyes trained on the man in front of her. Joseph did the same. "So, you're so hard up for entertainment you have to threaten kids to get your kicks?"

"Not hardly. I should have just killed the two of them, but I needed Billy. Now," Alan said, "move into the room with Kelly and over against that wall."

Catelyn moved first, obviously anxious to check on the unconscious girl. Joseph wracked his brain to try and figure a way out. He moved two steps in that direction.

Stopped.

"Wait a minute. We think we're pretty sure why you kept Billy alive. You needed him for the big game. I want to know about Tracy."

"Unfortunately, we don't always get what we want, now get in there."

Joseph narrowed his eyes. "You had money on this game, didn't you? You rigged it?"

Fury flashed in the man's eyes, and Joseph realized he'd nailed it.

"This girl needs a doctor," Catelyn interrupted. She glanced at her gun then back up at Joseph. He saw the intense worry on her face and knew he needed to move fast.

Alan Dillard refused to budge. Joseph tried again. "You killed Tracy, why?" He knew the answer but wanted to hear the man say it—and stall for backup to arrive. Where were they?

"I'm not playing the stall-for-time game. Now move." He fired the gun and the bullet pinged off the ceiling raining plaster on Kelly and Catelyn. She flinched, but never took her eyes from the man.

Joseph moved slightly, watching, waiting for Dillard to get a little closer—then dove for him, just as the man stepped back and fired again.

Catelyn screamed, "Joseph!"

The bullet kicked up the floor just under his armpit. He rolled again and surged to his feet. Alan leveled the gun at Joseph's head. "Don't move. I won't miss again."

Joseph froze.

He'd failed to take the man down. Where was their backup? He'd called it in about three minutes ago when he realized they might find Kelly stashed somewhere in this office.

The gun moved to center on Catelyn and Joseph felt nausea churn in his gut. "Stop!"

Catelyn eyed the gun from her perch next to Kelly. She turned her gaze on Joseph, her look speaking volumes. He was to do whatever it took to disarm this guy.

"You move again, and the lady cop gets it. You understand?"

Joseph swallowed hard, his heart pounding in his throat. He wanted this guy as bad as she did, but he wouldn't do a thing to place her in any more danger. He needed to stall. Surely, backup would be here soon.

"How did you get mixed up in this?"

"When our baseball program was close to being cut, I came up with the bright idea to form a gang, leaked some stories to the press about them and boom, we had money-hungry kids willing to break into houses and steal. Kids who thought being a part of a gang was cool."

"And of course you picked kids that had a psychological need. The need to be accepted, the need to feel like they're a part of a family, a group."

The man smirked. "Of course. Now into the room. I've got to get out of here."

"One more question." Joseph didn't give the man the option to refuse, he just asked it. "Why shoot Zachary?"

Startled, Alan jerked. Then he smiled and shrugged. "I didn't shoot Zachary."

"Who did?"

"I don't know and I don't care. Now move."

A siren sounded from outside and Alan cursed, his gaze moving toward the window.

And Joseph reacted, taking advantage of the split second distraction. He hit the floor and rolled for the man, hooking a hand around an ankle. The coach gave a startled yell as he went down, crashing into a filing cabinet before smacking the floor.

Joseph's senses took in Catelyn diving for her gun.

He flipped over and grabbed for Alan's wrist but not before the man managed to pull the trigger again. Plaster rained down as the two scrabbled across the floor.

Catelyn searched the floor for her gun. It had been kicked aside in the scuffle. She found it halfway under the bed. Snatching it up, she turned toward the action.

A bullet splattered the wall above her head and she ducked. Joseph was having a hard time subduing the angry man.

Finally, Joseph had the man's wrist pointed elsewhere and she was able to point her gun, yelling, "Freeze! Drop the weapon!"

Uniformed cops stormed the room, yelling for Dillard to let go of his gun.

And still the man fought. Catelyn lined up a shot. She didn't want to kill him, but she would if she had to. Then they rolled again. She lowered the gun, heart pounding, adrenaline surging.

She didn't dare pull the trigger when Joseph could make a sudden move; she might hit him. But if she didn't... Alan moved the gun around, leveling it with Joseph's head.

Catelyn pulled the trigger. And got him in the shoulder of his gun hand.

"Ah!" Alan jerked back, screaming, arms flailing, yet he still kept a grip on his weapon. Catelyn stepped forward and soccer-kicked his gun hand. Another pained yell escaped him and Joseph pinned him to the floor.

An officer moved in and helped cuff the enraged man. Bridges. He'd rejoined the action, obviously feeling the need to redeem himself.

Joseph, panting and gasping, rolled away and groaned. "Thank God."

Bridges stated over his radio, "Scene's clear."

The ambulance arrived and paramedics rushed in.

Catelyn pointed them to Kelly. Joseph wiped his eyes and took a deep breath. Concerned for him, she knelt beside him then offered him a hand up. "Are you all right?"

"I gotta get to the gym more," he grunted, ignoring her hand. "That guy's an ox."

Officers escorted the man to the nearest squad car. Right now he protested it was all a misunderstanding and he needed medical attention.

Catelyn snorted. Right. Watching the paramedics, she said, "I'm going to check on Kelly."

"I'm going to…sit here…one more minute."

Every muscle in his body quivered at the stress he'd just put it through. But satisfaction surged. They'd found Kelly and captured Tracy's killer. But what about Zachary? They still didn't know who'd shot the teen. Unless Alan was lying, which was a distinct possibility.

But for now, Alonso was right. His friend wasn't a murderer. He'd be pleased and Joseph would be his hero. Joseph smiled at the thought. More than likely, Alonso would ask him what took him so long.

Getting to his feet proved to be a painful process, but he did it with only a small grunt escaping his lips.

Now that he'd caught his breath, he had a few questions he wanted answered.

Catelyn moved back to him and he asked, "How's Kelly?"

"Drugged up, malnourished and will probably be in the hospital a while."

The crimes-scene unit entered and Catelyn greeted Sandy. "Hey, what are you doing working the field?"

"I decided I wanted a break from the lab. I'm trying my hand out here for a bit."

"Aw, Sandy, don't do that. Who am I going to call when I need a rush on evidence?"

Catelyn turned serious once more. "I'll be real interested in everything you find. We still have questions that need answers."

Joseph spoke up. "Yeah, like who shot Zachary Merritt."

"I want to search Alan Dillard's house."

"Sounds good. I'll request a team to get out there and do that right away."

"And I want to talk to Alan personally. Sounds like he had

a little side funny business going on with his female students. I'm willing to bet Tracy's not the first."

"Maybe not, but she's sure going to be the last."

At the hospital, Joseph and Catelyn hurried through the door and approached the front desk. Joseph obtained the information that Kelly was being admitted and that Alan's shoulder would require surgery. The bullet had lodged in his collar bone.

They decided to head for the waiting room. Catelyn nudged him. "Look."

"Stacy Dillard."

"Right. You want to talk to her or should I?"

Catelyn shrugged. "Maybe I should. She might relate better to a woman right now."

"Go ahead, I'll go see if my badge earns me any information."

Catelyn strolled over to the woman who sat staring out the window. "Mrs. Dillard?"

She jumped and turned, placing a hand over her heart. "Oh, you startled me."

"I'm so sorry about your husband."

"I'm not."

Ouch. Catelyn winced, but couldn't say she didn't understand the woman's bitterness—not if the woman was aware of her husband's extracurricular activities.

Stacy continued. "I'm not sorry about that. Sorry about a lot of other things, but not him."

"So you know about him and…"

"Tracy. Yes." She stood and crossed her arms. "I never thought him capable…and yet, I suppose I'm not terribly surprised, either."

"Why is that?"

"He's always had an eye for the young ones. I suppose after a while I just stopped wondering where he was and who he was with. I stopped caring."

"But you're here now waiting for him to get out surgery."

The woman drew in a deep breath. "Yes. Yes, I am. And as much as I might hate…well, let's just say he's still Alan Jr.'s father, right?"

Outwardly Catelyn nodded. On the inside, she was questioning everything. The woman had almost just practically admitted she hated her husband, yet here she sat waiting for the man to come out of surgery. Her son's father or not, that seemed strange to her. To each his own, she supposed.

"Mrs. Dillard?"

The two women turned as one. Stacy said, "Yes, Jill."

A blond nurse approached. "I just thought I'd let you know that Zachary's waking up. It's so sweet of you to be so concerned about him. His parents are with him now, but they gave me permission to pass the word to you."

Stacy Dillard drew in another deep breath. "Really? That's wonderful. When will I be able to see him?"

"Shortly, I suppose. The doctor's in with him now."

"Thank you so much."

Catelyn's brain hummed with this new information. "Great. Finally." She turned to the nurse. "Do you think he'll be able to tell us who shot him?"

"Oh, I think it'll be a while before he can talk. He's still on the ventilator, but I would hazard a guess that sometime tomorrow he'll be able to tell you what he knows about that day."

Another delay. Catelyn smiled her thanks and turned back to Stacy. "I'll be praying for your husband and family."

"Even though he's a terrible person?"

"God still loves him." Catelyn nearly choked on the words,

but knew they were true and maybe this woman needed to hear them. She was working on her anger, striving for the compassion she knew Jesus felt toward the man. Maybe if she gave lip service long enough, she'd actually feel it. Praying for the people she arrested was a new thing for her—and a tough one.

"Well, I don't need God right now, I need some news on Alan. I'd really like to know if he's going to live or die."

Catelyn blinked. She wasn't sure if the woman meant that to sound as cold as it did or if she was just still in shock over everything.

Giving her the benefit of the doubt, Catelyn shifted and watched Joseph pace back and forth, phone pressed to his ear.

"How's your son?"

"What?"

"Your son. He was sick when we came by earlier?"

"Oh, yes, he's better. Just a cold, I think." She grimaced. "I'll have to change his name just so he doesn't have to be ashamed of it." A huge sigh blew out of her. "He's with my mother right now. She'll keep him until I pick him up a little later. I don't know what I'd do without him. He's been my whole reason for…" She broke off and Catelyn handed her another tissue from the box on the table beside her.

Small talk over, Catelyn sat with the woman while Joseph pressed for answers from the CSU team. His brows rose at something said by the person on the other end of the line. Then he looked over at Catelyn and Stacy Dillard.

Crossing the room, he stopped in front of the woman. "Did Alan know that you were filing for divorce?"

EIGHTEEN

Joseph watched a number of expressions cross Mrs. Dillard's face. Fear, anger, resignation. She finally sighed and looked at the ceiling. "No, but I suppose you'll be talking to him about that when he comes out of surgery."

"Is there some reason you're waiting to let him in on your plan? The papers the crime-scene unit found were hidden pretty well and are dated three months ago."

"I…wanted to make sure I was making the right decision. Alan had threatened to take my son away if I ever left him. I had to make sure I was up for the fight." She gave an odd little smile. "But I guess today sort of clinched the deal. I can finally be free of his bullying and abuse, can't I? I can toss those divorce papers in his face. I don't have to worry about him anymore, do I?"

Compassion softened Joseph's face. "No, I guess you don't." He changed the subject and asked, "Zachary met with someone the day of his sister's funeral, but we can't figure out who that person was. Do you know if it was Alan and if he had a reason to want Zachary dead?"

Stacy shrugged and shifted her eyes to the door that separated her from her husband. "I don't know if they met or not. As far as if Alan had reason to want Zachary dead, it's possible. If Zachary found out about Alan's propensity for young high school girls, I'd say Alan would have some motive, wouldn't you?"

"Definitely. But did Zachary know?"

She leveled her gaze on him. "He knew. Zachary's been like a son, a troubled son, to me. He was angry with Alan for cheating on me. Zachary's the one who told me about Tracy."

"And you confronted Alan about this?"

"I did."

"What did he say?" Catelyn asked.

"Gave me a black eye and told me I had a good life. He said if I didn't want to lose it, I'd better be real careful about what I said and who I said it to."

"So, what did you do?"

"I kept my mouth shut and made divorce arrangements." Stacy used shaky fingers to pick at nonexistent lint on her faded blue jeans. "And I was working on a way to…get away from him. Forever."

"Then chickened out at the last minute?" Joseph pushed.

"No…" She paused. "Like I said, I just needed time."

"With your…friend?" There was no condemnation in his voice, but the woman still flinched.

"My *friend*—" she stressed the word "—is part of an underground organization that helps women and children get out of abusive situations. That's who Zachary saw me meeting with and interpreted it a different way. I couldn't tell him otherwise."

He stood. She was lying, but he wasn't sure why. It would take some digging to find out. "All right, Mrs. Dillard. Thanks for your cooperation. Let us know if there's anything we can do for you. It's a hard road you have ahead of you."

"Thank you."

Joseph and Catelyn moved to a separate area of the waiting room to continue to wait to hear about Alan and Kelly.

However, it looked like their timing might be just about perfect. According to the nurse, Zachary was showing very real signs of waking, so they decided to hang out and see if he came around enough to be able to tell them who shot him.

Catelyn said, "I guess since they're not taking the ventilator out until tomorrow, we could leave and come back."

"We could, but if he's responsive, we could at least get some yes or no answers to a few questions."

"True. He can also fingerspell anything he has to tell us."

"Right. I'm hoping he gives us a name."

She sat next to him and studied Alan's wife. She looked… hard. And worn down, sad and mad all at the same time. Like life had dealt her one blow too many.

The woman looked over at them and frowned, glanced at her watch, rose and headed for the exit. Probably had to pick up her son or something. Watching her leave, Catelyn asked Joseph, "Do you believe her?"

"What do you mean?"

"I don't know. She seems awfully eager to give up her husband." Catelyn chewed the thought.

Joseph pursed his lips. "He's done some pretty bad stuff to her. What about a woman scorned and all that?"

"Maybe."

"Why, you think she's lying?"

"I don't know. We've been lied to so much lately that I don't know that I'd recognize the truth if it bit me."

"Yeah, I know what you mean."

She looked at him. "Where was Alan during visitation for Tracy? Do you remember?"

"No, I just remember talking to his wife while standing in line. I never got to see who was sitting where. But I do remember she was looking for him. I wonder where she found him—*if* she found him?"

"We can ask her when she gets back." He moved closer to her and placed a hand over hers.

She jerked and looked at him. What was he doing?

"Catie, we need to talk."

Emotions swept over her at the tone in his voice. "No, we don't." Anger flooded her as she remembered him moving in front of her when they didn't know who was coming through the door of the gym. "You made yourself clear what you thought about me as a cop. Nothing more needs to be said. We're going to finish this case then go our separate ways. There. We talked."

"Okay, maybe I deserve that. But…"

"You say you have no problem with me being a cop yet you think I need protecting out there? Hello? It doesn't work that way. You have to have confidence in me."

"I know and I do."

"Well, you sure have a funny way of showing it! You stepped in front of me, Joseph. What does that say to you? It says tons to me."

Hard hands gripped her shoulders. "It says I care about you. It says I want to protect the woman I love."

Stunned, she couldn't react at first. He moved back a little, giving her some space. She couldn't believe he just said that. She remembered her father's definition of protection. He'd gotten so bad he hadn't wanted her mother to even leave the house. "I don't want that kind of love."

Joseph flinched and she realized she'd spoken her thoughts out loud. But he persisted. "Catie, you've got to understand. It wouldn't matter if you were a schoolteacher, I'd still want to protect you from some things. It's the way I'm wired. It's the way God made me. I won't apologize for it. If you'd been any other female cop in that hall with me, I never would've stepped in front of you. But…it was you."

"Which just clarifies why we aren't right for each other."

"No," he said. "No, it just means we can't *work* together. Sure, I might worry about you out working a case like any husband would, but that's normal. Can't you see that?"

She shook her head. "No, I really can't. All I can see are the fights, hear the yelling, the accusations, the harsh words. I don't know what normal is."

"Yes, you do. You've practically grown up in my parents' house. How can you say you don't know what normal is?"

Her mouth worked and nothing came out. Flashes of his parents, their disagreements handled in a totally different manner, their laughing, teasing one another, the support for each other in everything they did.

So opposite of everything her parents had stood for.

Could she possibly hope to be the kind of wife he wanted? Deserved? "But you want a wife who'll stay home, have dinner on the table every night, etcetera. I just can't promise that I can do that."

Her phone rang and Joseph leaned back with a groan. Snapping her attention to the phone, she answered the call, listened for a moment then hung up. She looked up at Joseph and forced herself to see the man as only her partner right now. Told herself to ignore the longing she still saw in his gaze. Finally he cleared his throat and narrowed his eyes. "What?"

"CSU found the gun they think was used to shoot Zachary."

"Found it in Alan's house is my guess."

"Right."

"Well, I suppose that answers that question. Alan Dillard shot Zachary."

"Excuse me, officers?"

They both looked up at the nurse. She said, "Zachary is awake. His parents said that you could come in and see him if you'd like."

NINETEEN

When they entered the room, Zachary looked rough. Various tubes extended from him and monitors clicked and beeped. But at least his eyes were open. They widened when he spotted them. His heart rate picked up and Joseph said, "We're sure glad you're awake."

The boy lifted a weak hand to sign, "Yes."

"We're also hoping you can tell us who shot you. Do you know who?"

"Maybe."

Catelyn stepped forward, intensity radiating from her. "Can you spell his name."

His fingers moved, slowly, but with clarity. H-E-R.

"Her?" Catelyn glanced at Joseph and frowned. Then went wide with understanding. "It was a woman?"

Another signed yes.

"It wasn't Alan Dillard?"

"No." His fingers moved as in slow motion.

"Who? Do you know who?"

His eyes shut and his mother moved in to touch his hand. "Zachary, please, honey. Try to stay awake. Tell them who did this to you."

Zachary's lids fluttered. Closed, then opened once more.

Joseph pressed, "Who was it, Zachary?"

Fingers slowly formed the individual letters to spell: D-I-L-L-A-R-D.

Joseph blinked. Maybe the kid had been confused when he spelled H-E-R. "Alan Dillard? He's in surgery as we speak."

Zachary's eyes drooped, then closed. Joseph patted the kid's hand, but he was back out cold.

Joseph looked at Catelyn. "Let's see if Mrs. Dillard is back in the waiting room and ask her a few questions."

Catelyn shook her head. "He specifically spelled H-E-R. What if Stacy heard Zachary was waking up? What if she wasn't here to see her husband, what if she was waiting to finish the job?"

"I don't know. What reason would she have to want Zachary dead?" He addressed the question to Zachary's parents.

Both looked shocked at the recent developments and Mrs. Merritt said, "I don't know. I know my children were mixed up in that gang. I…didn't want to admit it at first, but I can't really deny it at this point." She looked down at her son. "I guess my husband and I've been so focused on our careers, we lost sight of what we were working so hard for…our family."

Joseph felt a pang of sympathy for the woman. Her husband ran a hand down the side of his face and grunted. "Well, we've got a second chance with Zachary and Justin. As soon as we can, we're going to have a family meeting and get some things straightened out." He frowned and glanced at the door. "I have a hard time believing Stacy Dillard shot my son. She's been nothing but kind and caring toward him."

"Your son is the one who told her that her husband was having an affair with a fellow student."

"What? Zachary wouldn't do that. He worshipped the ground Alan Dillard walked on—and he didn't care much for Stacy. He said Alan deserved a better wife than her. If the man was having an affair and Zachary learned of it, there's no way he would have said anything to her, not out of concern for her feelings, but because of Alan."

"You know, I felt Stacy was lying to us at the hospital. She's the one that pulled the trigger."

Calling for a car to go by the Dillard house and see if Mrs. Dillard went home and orders to pick her up if she did, Joseph then asked Catelyn, "Are you ready to track this woman down?"

"Absolutely."

They left with promises to call as soon as they knew anything and Mr. and Mrs. Merritt agreed to get as much information out of Zachary as soon as he woke up again.

Joseph watched Catelyn exit the door ahead of him and knew his time with her was running short. They needed to get this case solved so they could get back to resolving the situation between them once and for all. *Lord, help us please?*

The drive to the Dillard house was silent. The woman hadn't been in the waiting room when they'd returned to the area. A call from the cruiser sent to check her house confirmed the woman wasn't there. either.

"Her son," Catelyn blurted.

"What?"

"If she's going to make a run for it, she'd probably grab her kid first." *At least that's what I'd do*. But what kind of mother was Stacy Dillard? She had a feeling the woman's child was everything to her. "She said her mother had her son. We need to find out who her mother is and where she lives."

Joseph got on the radio and started the process to find out the information they needed. A call to the child's elementary school principal found him at home on this Sunday afternoon. He instantly provided the woman's name.

Cheryl Frazier.

Within minutes, Joseph had the address and, with siren wailing, headed in the direction that would take them to the west side of town. He also had back-up units on the way.

Catelyn watched the scenery whiz by. A middle-class neighborhood came in to view. She shut the siren off and Joseph wheeled in. They found the house without incident. She just prayed Stacy and her son were still here. They pulled up to the curb and quickly assessed the scene before them.

"Looks quiet," Catelyn observed.

"Looks can be deceiving," he answered, scanning the front of the well-maintained home. "Be ready for anything. This woman shot a teenager."

"I wonder what he did that had her pulling that trigger. Somehow I don't buy the story she fed us at the hospital. And yet, she was in front of us in the line at the funeral." Confusion crimped her. "I just don't see how she would have had time to get up to the balcony, get her gun ready and shoot Zachary."

"She left to find her husband."

"Then came back to talk to the people in front of us, remember?"

"Yes, I do. So, maybe Zachary didn't run because of our presence, he saw her and took off."

She shrugged and unclipped her shoulder holster. "It's a theory, but I still don't see how she made it up to the balcony in time to shoot him. And how would she know he was going to run out of the mortuary?"

He pulled out his phone. "I don't know. All good questions. Let's see if anyone answers the number here so we can get those questions answered."

Dialing the number, he waited. Two more cruisers pulled in next to the curb, their sirens silenced, not wanting to further upset an already possibly frantic woman.

Joseph slipped the phone back into his pocket. "No one's answering."

"You want to do the honors?" she asked, motioning to the door. Joseph stepped up on the porch and knocked.

The window next to him exploded in a crash of flying glass. He ducked out of the way, to the side, the glass missing him by millimeters. "Hey! Police! Freeze!"

Another gunshot sounded. Then a small voice, "Mommy! Mommy!"

Catelyn spun herself up against the side of the house away from the broken window, heart pounding. "Joseph, are you okay?"

"Yeah, fine. We've got to get that gun away from whoever's in there."

"I don't want to start shooting back, there's a kid in there."

"Absolutely." Gun held pointing up, he yelled, "Mrs. Dillard, I need you to throw your weapon out."

"No!" A trembling voice came from inside. It sounded close to the window, to Catelyn's left and they could hear her clearly. "Mrs. Dillard, is that you?"

"No, it's Cheryl Frazier, Stacy's mother, and you need to leave now."

Catelyn shot a look at Joseph and mouthed. "The mother?"

He shrugged. "Zachary was pretty out of it. Maybe he was trying to spell Mrs. Dillard's mother. Who knows?"

Right now it didn't matter. At least Mrs. Frazier was talking. Always a good sign. If she was talking, she wasn't hurting anyone. "Where's your daughter and grandson?"

"In here with me. They're safe. My poor Stacy…she's just not in her right mind right now. She's had too much put on her with everything. We're taking Alan Jr. and we're leaving, do you understand? We've worked so hard…" A muffled sob broke through.

Catelyn spoke up. "Ma'am, you know we can't let you do that."

"Then I'll…I'll…I don't know what I'll do, but…something."

They needed a hostage negotiator. Catelyn shifted and licked her lips. "Your grandson's listening to you, isn't he?"

Shifting, a scrape. Catelyn tensed, felt the butt of her gun against her palm. She really didn't want to shoot anyone, especially not Alan Jr.'s grandmother.

"Yes."

"You don't want to scare him, do you?"

Sniffling, a moment of weeping. "It wasn't supposed to be like this."

Looking around, she spotted the two uniformed officers who'd arrived at the home just minutes after she and Joseph pulled in.

And Ethan O'Hara.

She gave a small wave to the man who was her usual partner and was Joseph's brother-in-law.

Ethan waved back and motioned to Joseph he'd help cover him. Joseph looked surprised to see Ethan, but nodded for her to keep talking. He was going around the back of the house. He held up two fingers.

She nodded, two taps on his radio would mean he was inside. She'd continue talking to Cheryl Frazier and pray she could remember everything she'd ever learned about hostage negotiations until a trained negotiator arrived.

"How was it supposed to be, Cheryl?" She used the woman's first name, hoping it would keep her focused on the conversation and not on whatever Joseph and Ethan were doing around back.

Another sniffle. "I just wanted to get us away."

"Why?"

"Because I'm so ashamed of my son-in-law, so hurt, so *mad* at him for what he's done to Stacy and Alan Jr. How could he do that to them? To his own son?" Cheryl's fury exploded from her as she spat the words.

Catelyn flinched at the venom in the woman's voice. "I understand. It was a terrible thing he did. A total betrayal of their vows, their trust. And an ugly legacy to leave behind for Alan Jr." Mention the kid as often as possible. Keep her mind on her grandson—and the fact that he needs her.

"Yes! Yes it was."

Joseph crept up to the back door and tried the handle.

Locked. Of course.

Ethan stayed behind, covering him.

Joseph moved through the shrubbery trying the windows. Finally, the last one on the end lifted. A quick glance inside told him the room was empty. Hoisting himself in, he landed silently on the carpeted floor and looked around. This must be where Alan Jr. slept when he visited. A twin bed with a puppy-dog bedspread sat against one wall with a little white dresser beside it.

"What are Stacy and Alan Jr. going to do if you go to jail, Cheryl? He's already lost his father. What's he going to do if you get arrested or—worse? You said your daughter's not in her right mind. That leaves you to care for the boy. Do you have another family member who can keep Alan Jr.?" he heard Catelyn ask. Her voice carried through the broken window.

Dead silence from the house.

Joseph slid down the hall toward the den where the action was taking place. Where was the kid? The mother?

It was a typical ranch-style house and a quick sweep showed all three bedrooms and hall bathroom to be empty. So that left the kitchen, dining and den areas.

The end of the hall opened up into the den. He could see Stacy sitting on the couch holding a little boy on her lap.

"Mom, put the gun down, please." The woman had her eyes trained on her mother. Tears stood out on her cheeks and she raised a palm to brush them off.

"Stacy, you just hush. I'm taking care of you, just like I always have." Her mother never turned from the window.

Joseph stepped inside the den then to the right into the living room so he couldn't be spotted. He needed to get Stacy's attention so he could get her and the boy out of there. Assuming she wouldn't turn him in.

A chance he'd have to take. He waited until she turned her head slightly, then stepped into her peripheral vision. She started and he raised a finger to his lips. Her eyes narrowed, then shot to her mother, who stood staring out the window. Her mouth opened as though to call out and Joseph raised his gun a tad. If the woman turned from the window to shoot at him, he'd have no choice.

Sorrow crossed Stacy's features but she clamped her lips together and didn't give him away.

Instead, she shifted her son and rose with him on her hip. He wrapped his arms around her neck and leaned his head on her shoulder. He looked scared stiff at the upheaval going on.

Cheryl whirled and Joseph jerked back. "Stacy, what are you doing?"

"Going into the kitchen. I need to give Alan Jr. his medicine."

"Leave Alan Jr. there. On the couch."

Stacy paused, then sighed and set him down. He clung to her and said, "Don't leave me."

Grief spasmed her features. "All right, baby, I'll stay with you."

Joseph sucked in a relieved breath. She hadn't given away

his location yet. And they were still in the line of fire. She'd been trying to get the boy away from them, trying to open up the opportunity for Joseph to get Cheryl.

The child hadn't seen him, so hopefully he would stay put on the couch. He reached around his mother to pick up a stuffed turtle, clutching it close while never taking his eyes from his grandmother and the gun.

Joseph stayed put behind the cover of the wall, tapping his radio twice to let Catelyn know he was in. She tapped back once. Good, she got his message.

"Cheryl," he said. The woman whirled to stare at him in shock.

"How did you get in here?" she demanded.

He ignored her. "Why did you shoot Zachary?"

Catelyn figured her negotiating time had run out. Joseph was inside. She raced the few remaining steps to the broken window, doing her best to stay out of the line of fire should someone decide to send another bullet that way.

She knew Ethan had Joseph's back.

Officers swarmed the house, weapons drawn.

Looking through the window, Catelyn saw the woman was distracted, noticed Joseph watching. Slowly, she reached through the broken window and silently unlatched it and raised it in one smooth movement. She slipped in and landed in the den—and came face-to-face with Cheryl Frazier as she whirled toward the noise. "Drop your gun, Cheryl."

Tears of frustration streamed down the woman's cheeks. Alan Jr. sat on his mother's lap, his little hands covering his ears, eyes squeezed shut, as he rocked back and forth. Catelyn softened her voice. "Your family needs you, Cheryl. Don't add anything else to your list of things to fight."

Stacy begged, "Stop, Mama. I need you. Alan Jr. needs you. Look around you. You can't fight them and win."

The hand holding the pistol shook. Cheryl drew in a steadying breath. "Get them out of here." She motioned to Stacy and Alan Jr.

Catelyn gave the order to the officers. Immediately, they ushered the two out of the house. The woman started moving toward the kitchen, the gun held out in front of her not aimed at anyone. Yet.

"Ma'am, I really need you to stop and put the gun down."

"I really didn't want to hurt anyone. I was just taking care of my family, just like I always have."

Ethan appeared in the hallway. He looked at Catelyn and she could almost read his mind. He had a clean shot. She shook her head.

Joseph held his gun steady as he moved with the woman. "I understand that, ma'am. You were just protecting your family. But we can't resolve any of this as long as you hold on to that gun." Cheryl stepped into the kitchen, still facing Joseph and now Ethan.

Catelyn stepped next to Joseph so she could see the woman. "Cheryl, what are doing? You need to put the gun down."

"I didn't want to get blood on the carpet." She spoke casually and it didn't occur to Catelyn what she meant until she swung the gun up to rest the business end against her temple.

"Stop!"

Joseph had gone to his knees the moment the gun started moving. Ethan had pulled back around the corner against the wall and Catelyn had done the same move with the opposite wall. Now she realized what Cheryl meant when she said she didn't want to get blood on the carpet. Kitchen linoleum was much easier to clean up.

For a brief moment, the woman's face morphed into Catelyn's father's. She blinked. Joseph, still on his knees, kept his gun aimed just in case Mrs. Frazier decided to swing her weapon around and point it at him.

And Catelyn wanted to step in front of him.

The feeling stunned her; shook her to the core and swept her entire being with nausea.

She pushed it away. They had one more thing to deal with. "Mrs. Frazier, why did you shoot Zachary?"

Mrs. Frazier's gun hand shook, tremor after tremor. Catelyn prayed she wouldn't spasm and pull the trigger. "He was going to tell Alan that Stacy was going to divorce him. Alan Dillard was that boy's hero. He never knew…"

"He never knew what Alan was, right? He never knew what was going on between Alan and Tracy? And he never told Stacy that Alan was having an affair, did he? She lied to us in the hospital to protect you, didn't she?"

"Yes, she lied. I think Tracy tried to tell Zachary that Alan wasn't all he was cracked up to be, but the boy just wouldn't listen. And when Stacy came home…the day of the visitation, right before the visitation…she was hysterical."

Joseph asked, "Why?"

"She'd met with Zachary and tried to reason with him. He wouldn't have any part of it. He was going to tell Alan the next time he saw him."

"And Stacy was afraid of Alan's reaction?"

The gun lowered a tad as her elbow drooped. Her arm was getting tired. Keep her talking, Joseph.

"Stacy was afraid of Alan, period."

"He was abusive."

With a tight jaw, the woman nodded. "In every way imaginable. But when Alan went after Alan Jr.…."

Catelyn winced—every mother's nightmare. "She'd had enough."

Her arm trembled, the gun shifted. "He threatened to take

Alan Jr. from her and never let her see him again." A harsh laugh escaped her. "And I have no doubt he would have followed through with it. Stacy tried to find help, even went to the police to see what she could do."

"Why is there no record of this on file? We did an extensive background check on Alan."

"Did you come across who Alan's favorite poker buddy was?" she snapped.

"No."

"Try Mayor McCloud."

Understanding darkened Catelyn's brain. She made a mental note to do a little research into Mayor McCloud's life. She watched the gun in the woman's hand. It was almost pointing to the ceiling at this stage. She was so busy telling her story, she wasn't paying attention to the weapon. Just a little bit more and she could…

"So, Zachary and Stacy met the afternoon of the visitation. Stacy tried to talk him out of telling Alan about the divorce. But, wait a minute…how did Zachary know about it in the first place?"

"That stupid kid went over to my Stacy's house looking for Alan one afternoon after his sister was killed. Just walked right in. Stacy was in the kitchen going over the papers. Zachary saw them and stormed out with Stacy yelling at him not to tell, that she was just thinking about it and didn't really mean it."

"So she came to you, and you decided to take care of the situation."

She closed her eyes as though pained at the memory.

And Catelyn struck.

She gave a flying tackle and clipped the woman around the knees. Shrieking, Mrs. Frazier went down, Catelyn landing on top of her.

Joseph was beside them in a heartbeat, kicking the weapon

aside. Ethan grabbed her arms and pinned them behind her back.

And then all the fight went out of her.

Panting, Catelyn rose to her feet and helped Joseph pull the weeping Mrs. Frazier to hers. Ethan went to tell everyone that it was over.

Catelyn said, "Just one more question, how did you get off the balcony of the funeral home without anyone seeing you?"

Tears dripped off the woman's chin and she sniffed. "It was so easy. I simply crawled into one of the coffins in the room off the balcony. There were plenty to choose from." Hands now cuffed behind her back, she shrugged. "I chose an empty one."

Joseph spoke up. "You used Alan's gun to shoot Zachary. How did you get your hands on it and how did it wind up back at his house? Our CSU guys found it."

"I have a key to the house. I simply went by when no one was home. I was hoping you would find the gun and blame the shooting on Alan."

Catelyn shook her head. Oh, what a tangled web we weave…

Now that the case was officially closed, Catelyn had one last thing to take care of. She had to decide if she was strong enough to love a cop—and if she could be the kind of wife Joseph wanted.

She finally admitted it to herself.

She loved Joseph. Had loved him for a long time.

But did she love him enough?

She wanted to. And that scared her and yet thrilled her all at the same time. And Sandy was right. She and Joseph did have something her parents had neglected from the start of their relationship.

God.

But could she quit her job for him? She just didn't know.

She dreaded the next item on her to-do list for the day, yet was determined to get through it. *Please, Jesus, I need Your strength.*

She thought she heard someone call her name, but not in the mood for conversation, she ignored it and continued on like she hadn't heard. Climbing into her car, she cranked it and took off. In the rearview mirror, she could see Joseph standing in the parking lot, hand raised.

Guilt hammered her. That was really rude. She was going to have to talk to him at some point. But she just wasn't ready for the conversation she knew he wanted to have.

And she wanted to be ready.

I could have just talked to the man. Told him I needed some space. Lord, what do I do? What do You want? I'm so messed up inside over my parents, I just don't know if I can ever have a normal relationship with another cop. Especially an over-protective one. But I do know what I need to do right now. I need to let go of my anger, Lord. I need to let it go and I need Your help to do that.

She picked up her phone and punched in Joseph's number. He answered on the first ring. "Hey."

"I'm sorry."

"For?"

"For ignoring you in the parking lot. I just…I've got something I need to do and I…want to do it alone."

"All you had to do was say something." She winced at the hurt in his voice.

"I know. I had a brief moment of cowardice. That's why I'm calling. I owed you an apology."

"Apology accepted. So when do you think you'll be ready to talk?"

"Soon, okay?"

"Do you want me to come with you wherever you're going?"

She thought about what she was going to do. "Yes. No. I'm not sure."

He gave a small laugh. "Okay, that's clear."

Heaving a sigh, Catelyn turned to make her way through the gates of the cemetery. Winding around the narrow paths, she said, "I guess not. Maybe I need to do this on my own. Face my demon, so to speak."

"Call me when you're done?"

"Yes. Yes, I will."

"All right. See you soon."

She hung up and turned right. She'd only been here one other time, the day of the funeral, but the way to her father's grave was permanently embedded in her mind.

Parking to the side, she slowly climbed from her vehicle. Not really sure why she felt the need to do this to herself, she kept a prayer on her lips as she made her way over to the grave.

Someone had left fresh flowers. Who? A buddy from the force, no doubt.

Catelyn knelt, not caring if the grass left a stain on the knees of her faded jeans. She touched the headstone. Traced the words that had been carved into it.

Harold James Clark. Family man and devoted defender of the peace. Gone too early.

Yeah. Too early. Well, whose fault is that?

Then the grief hit her.

And the memories flooded her. The good ones. Ones she hadn't thought about in over a decade. The ones that had been overshadowed by the anger she felt toward the man who'd given up and killed himself. The ones recorded in the "fun book" she'd taken to her mother the day after they'd arrested Cheryl Frazier.

"Oh, Daddy," she whispered, "I miss you."

She closed her eyes and let the tears fall. She'd been his pride and joy when she'd been small, riding on his shoulders, laughing, giggling and wearing his uniform hat.

Why was she just now remembering this?

She remembered the swing in their big backyard. He'd pushed her to the sky, so high her toes could "touch God."

She remembered his big booming voice every day, the minute he walked in the door. "Gimme a hug, kiddo!" And she'd run to him and he'd swing her up in his big muscular arms and squeeze the breath out of her. She remembered her mother watching the two of them and smiling. Catelyn let out a sob. She remembered her mother *smiling*. *Oh, thank you, God, for that.*

The rush of memories tripped over themselves in her mind, stealing the hate and anger from her heart.

Not caring if she looked like a fool, not concerned about who might be watching, she leaned forward and wrapped her arms around the cold headstone, wishing it was her daddy's warm hard chest. She lay her head against the smoothly carved words and pretended she could hear his heart beating one last time. Pretended she could feel his arms wrapped around her in one last breath-stealing squeeze.

"I've hated you for so long, been so filled with anger that I'm not sure how to do this, but I hope this is a start." She took a deep breath, smelled the scent of freshly turned dirt, a hint of rain and felt the possibility of the sun as it struggled to peek through the clouds. "I forgive you, Daddy. I have to. It's the only way I'm going to be able to love someone of my own. It's the only way I'll ever have peace."

Tears dripped to the soft green earth. The wind blew, and time passed as she prayed and talked to her dad. Finally, bones creaking and muscles aching, she let go of the headstone—and her anger—to sit back on her heels and caress the letters etched into the head stone. "I love you, Daddy, and I miss you."

She raised her eyes toward heaven and let the tears continue to fall.

Joseph stood against his vehicle, arms folded across his chest as he watched the scene play out before him. Never had he witnessed such an outpouring of grief. He felt like an intruder. And yet he couldn't leave her. She might need him.

Right, he mocked himself, when has she ever needed you?

But she might—this time.

Hopefully.

Anxiety tightened his gut as he watched her weep, her silent tears nearly ripping his heart out. And when she'd wrapped her arms around the headstone, he couldn't stand it and had to turn away from the scene.

Forcing himself not to go to her, he let her have her moments with her father, praying, crying out that somehow God would give her the peace she so desperately needed.

Finally, he turned back to see her sitting on her heels, mopping up her face, the emotional devastation of the storm passed.

He took several steps in her direction, then stopped, wondering if he should intrude. Wondering if she needed more time.

She pushed herself up to her feet, and he closed the gap placing his hands on her shoulders.

Catelyn didn't even jump as she felt a pair of hands lightly fall on her shoulders. She'd smelled Joseph's cologne, a woodsy, masculine scent that she never tired of, about thirty seconds ago and knew he stood behind her.

Shuddering, broken and yet finally at peace, she felt cleansed. Ready to make a new start in life.

But was Joseph the right person to make that start with?

She hoped so.

As long as he understood some things.

Sucking in a deep breath, she turned, looked into his eyes—and nearly felt her knees buckle at the look of love shining there. Tears of sympathy glistened, and she simply wanted to melt into his arms and let the world fade away.

Oh, Lord, help me.

He smiled. "Hey, can I do anything to help?"

"You followed me—again," she said, referencing the nursing home incident. "And it's the second time you've found me in tears."

"I want to be there for you, Catelyn."

She swallowed hard. "I know you do, Joseph, but I don't know that you can do that without wanting to protect me. I don't want to compare you to my father, but…" She shoved her hands in the back pockets of her jeans and started walking.

Joseph followed her behind her. "Catelyn, I'm not your father."

"You stepped in front of me. A fellow cop. And one with a gun at that. What if I'd chosen to pull the trigger at that moment?" She shuddered at the thought.

"You wouldn't have. You're too good a cop."

"Then why did you feel the need to step in front of me?" she demanded.

"Catelyn, I told you I wasn't protecting the cop. I was protecting the woman I love." He ran a hand through his dark hair, causing a sprig to stand up. "Excuse me for that being a crime."

"Oh, Joseph, it's not a crime. It's…it's…"

"What I'm supposed to do. I'm wired that way, both by God and by my upbringing. I could no more let you stand in the path of a bullet than I could sprout wings and fly. I don't know what else to say to convince you."

And it hit her. She remembered in the house when he was in the line of fire. She remembered the urge she felt to step in front of him, get him out of the path should the woman decide to pull the trigger.

Why? Because she loved him. Would she have felt that way if it had been another cop standing there?

No.

Suddenly, she saw things in a different light, from a whole different perspective. His perspective.

He loved her. Really, truly, loved her.

Loved her enough to step in front of a bullet for her.

Loved her enough to die for her.

Just like she felt for him.

Excitement swirled within her. "How can we make this work?"

"Well, we can't work together, that's for sure."

She choked out a laugh. "Okay."

"You've been under the impression that I don't want you to be a cop. And I'll admit, two years ago you that would have been the case. But recently, I've been thinking, praying, picturing us together…and I realize I tried to make you into someone you're not. And that's okay, but I fell in love with who you are, not who I wanted you to be."

She sucked in a hiccupping sob and tried to speak, but he placed a finger over her lips, so she'd kept quiet. He went on, "I'll worry about you while you're on duty, but I don't think I'll obsess about it. I'd appreciate it if you would check in with me when you can. And I'll be sure to do the same with you."

Surprise lit her eyes. "You'd do that?"

"Well, sure, why wouldn't I?"

"My father told my mother what he was doing was none of her concern and would get furious if she even suggested that he check in with her and…"

He grasped her upper arms and pulled her closer. "Aw, Catie, I'm really not like your father. I love you, I love the Lord. We'll rely on Him to get us through the rough times and rejoice with Him through the good times. It's true that all my life I figured I'd marry a woman like my mother. And then God dropped you into my life. A woman completely opposite from Mom is some ways…and yet very similar in all the ways that matter. Especially when it comes to loving the Lord. I'm fine with you being a cop, I promise."

Tears clogged her throat. "You're a very good man, Joseph."

"And you're an amazing woman who's been harboring a lot of anger for a long time."

"Huh. You noticed that, did you?"

"Yeah, I noticed."

Catelyn took a deep breath. "Well, I…think it's been bubbling beneath the surface for a while. Ever since my father shot himself, I've been…afraid."

"Of?"

"Of being abandoned."

This time it was Joseph's turn to suck in a swift breath. "Aw, Catie…and I…"

"Yes, when you left me two years ago, it just about killed me."

He flinched, her words wounding him with their honesty. She held up a hand and said, "But you were right to do what you did. I was too…insecure. I kept waiting for you to leave me and that's no way to have a relationship. My father said he loved me, then he killed himself. I was begging God to intervene with my mother and He didn't seem to be listening. And then you…you were too good to be true. I couldn't believe someone like you could love someone like me." She gave a small laugh. "I had some real self-esteem issues didn't I?"

"But I never saw those. You always seemed so confident, so in charge, so…"

"Bullheaded?"

"You said it, not me." He quirked a smile and was relieved when he got one in return.

"Right. Bullheaded. Anyway, when you left, it just confirmed what I'd been afraid of all along. I told myself I was better off, that if you hadn't left when you did, you'd leave me eventually."

"But I didn't want to."

"I know. I drove you away. And it was probably for the best at the time. It made me realize that God was still in control. That no matter what was happening with my life, no matter how far away I thought He was, He was still there, just waiting on me to come back to Him. And I had to trust Him with you."

"And He brought me back."

"Much to my dismay at the time."

"I was never so happy to accept an assignment as this one. Oh, I fought it at first, especially after I heard who my partner was going to be, but then I saw you standing there by the crime scene…and those two years just kind of faded away and I wanted back what we'd had—and more."

She nodded, the tears now dripping from her chin. "Me, too," she whispered.

"I love you, Catie. Will you marry me this time if I promise to refuse to work with you?"

Laughing, she reached up to encircle his neck with her arms. "I will."

"Good." He leaned down and met her lips with his, relishing the feeling of coming home. There'd never been another woman for him and he'd missed her desperately during his time in New York; now he reveled in the knowledge that she loved him as fully as he loved her.

He lifted his head a bit and looked down at her. "When?"

"When what?"

"When will you marry me?"

"Um…soon?"

"Yeah, soon is what I kind of had in mind." He touched the tip of his nose to hers.

"I want my mom to be there."

"Absolutely."

She pulled his head back down for another tingling kiss.

Yeah, he'd definitely come home.

To stay.

* * * * *

Dear Reader,

This story was such a blessing to write. Thank you for joining me as we met up with the Santino family once again. What a great group of brothers and sisters we have here who all love the Lord—and the special people He picked out just for them.

Catelyn had such a deep anger left over from her childhood, and as a result, while she still prayed to God, she felt distant from Him. Once she got that resolved, she found a new, deeper relationship with Him—and was able to let herself love Joseph the way he deserved to be loved. I pray that you are walking closely with the God who loved you enough to die for you. Let Him wrap His arms around you and bring hope, joy and peace into your life.

I love to hear from my readers. If you get a chance, drop me an e-mail and let me know what you think about Catelyn and Joseph. My e-mail address is lynetteeason@lynetteeason.com and my snail mail is P.O. Box 2212, Spartanburg, SC 29304.

God bless and until next time…

Lynette Eason

QUESTIONS FOR DISCUSSION

1. What are your thoughts about the story in general? Did it move fast enough for you?

2. What do you think about Catelyn's attitude toward Joseph? Do you think she walked away from a good man too soon? What should she have done differently?

3. Do you understand her reluctance to get involved with Joseph once again? Have you ever dealt with a relationship like that? What did you do?

4. What was your favorite scene in the story? Why?

5. Was there a scene you didn't like? Why?

6. How would you describe Catelyn's relationship with God? Joseph's?

7. What do you think about Catelyn's sudden realization that she'd just plain mad at God? How did she handle that realization and do you think she responded the way God wanted her to?

8. What do you think about forgiveness? Catelyn had some work cut out for her in order to forgive her parents for their selfishness during her childhood. Is there someone you need to forgive?

9. Why did Catelyn become a cop? Do you think it helped

her to understand her parents any better? Or would she have been better off choosing a different career path?

10. Did you figure out who the "bad guys" were? If so, what gave them away?

11. Joseph's father makes it a point to say that Catelyn isn't like Joseph's mother, but she's a good woman and "a man could consider himself blessed with a girl like that." Are you the type of woman that is a blessing? How can you be that woman?

12. Rearing kids in today's world is particularly scary once they start getting older and can be gone from your sight for extended periods of time. If you're a parent, what have you done to ensure that your children know right from wrong and have the ability to make wise decisions?

13. What attributes does Joseph have as a man and a cop that make him the perfect match for Catelyn?

14. Joseph cleared Dylan's name and became a hero to his younger brother, Alonso. Who is your hero and why?

15. Catelyn is finally able to put her past behind her with Joseph's and God's help. Is there something you need to put aside in order to have a healthy relationship with someone that you care about?

Private investigator Wade Sutton plans to hightail it out of Dry Creek long before December 25. The town holds too many *unmerry* memories. Until he's asked to watch over a woman in danger, a woman whose faith changes him forever.

Turn the page for a sneak preview of
SILENT NIGHT IN DRY CREEK
by Janet Tronstad.
Available in October 2009
from Love Inspired®

Wade wished he had never come back to Dry Creek. Or, since he had come back, he wished people hadn't been so kind to him. Barbara making that cake for him was putting him off his game. And then Jasmine—usually he didn't have any trouble taking a tough line with a suspect. But then, he'd never been tempted to kiss a suspect before.

He watched Jasmine's back as she walked to the table. She was ramrod straight and angry with him. He knew he'd come on too strong, but it was either that or forgetting everything he knew about law enforcement and refusing to believe she could be responsible for anything.

As a lawman he had to consider all the possibilities, and it was hard to forget that Lonnie had been her partner. She could have sent him a coded message that in some way had helped him escape from prison, or at least given him an incentive to risk everything to get outside.

He wished he knew how to look into the heart of a person so he would know what Jasmine was thinking. Was she as innocent as she looked, or as guilty as she had been the first time she was convicted of a crime? He knew better than most how many ex-cons fell back into theft. He was often the one who took them in the second time around and listened to their sorry excuses.

"I gave you the biggest piece of cake," Barbara said as he sat down at his place at the table.

"Thank you." Wade smiled. It was the cake of his childhood fantasies, and he was going to have to force himself to eat it. All he wanted to do was take Jasmine home and then park his car at the end of the lane to her father's place. Why did she have to be tied up with Lonnie? Why couldn't she be a nice, ordinary woman like Barbara here? Carl never had to worry about arresting *her*.

Wade felt the smoothness of the cake on his tongue and the sweet tang of the raspberry filling. He smiled up at Barbara and thanked her again for the cake. The two kids at the table were smacking their lips and demanding more, just as Wade would be doing if he wasn't so troubled.

Then he looked down the table and saw his dear friend Edith. She wouldn't be happy about him keeping an eye on anyone. It was clear the older woman was very fond of Jasmine. That, of course, was the problem with being a lawman and trying to have friends. He liked things black and white with no shades of gray. He didn't want to have feelings for the suspect.

By doing his job, he was going to upset Jasmine and everyone else in Dry Creek. For the first time since he'd driven into town, he missed the barren feel of his apartment in Idaho Falls. He knew who he was there.

It didn't take long for Wade to leave the Walls' house, with Jasmine walking in front of him. The night was cold. Jasmine wrapped her arms around her body to keep warm and hurried to his car. He was still nursing that leg of his, so he went more slowly than she did. He made it in good time, though, and as he opened the car door for her, she nodded her thanks and slid into the passenger seat.

The first thing Wade did after he got into the car was to

move the dial up on the heater. Snowflakes were just starting to fall, but they were scattered enough that he could clear them away with his windshield wipers.

He silently turned his car around and started down the sheriff's lane. The car lights shone on the falling snow, making the flakes look like pinpricks in the darkness.

"You don't think Lonnie would do something to my father, do you?" Jasmine asked. She looked up at him with eyes full of worry. "Lonnie's not very stable. I wouldn't want anyone around here to be hurt by him."

Wade shrugged. "With all you'd inherit if Elmer were out of the picture—"

Jasmine gasped. "I don't care about the money."

"Lonnie might."

That turned her quiet. He didn't want her to worry, though.

"He won't even have the chance to get close to anyone," Wade assured her. "We'll have the feds all over the place by tomorrow. Lonnie has a better chance of breaking into Fort Knox than he has of sneaking into Dry Creek."

Wade hoped he wasn't lying. He had no idea what the feds would do. And they might have some completely different theories as to why Lonnie had broken out of prison. It might have nothing at all to do with Jasmine or anyone in Dry Creek.

"You'll be safe," Wade said as he opened his door.

He walked around to the passenger door and opened it. Wade stood by the open car door and watched as Jasmine pulled her coat closer to her body. She wasn't making any move to walk toward the house and he wasn't making any move to let her. Finally Wade reached out and touched her cheek. It was soft and a little damp. She must have been crying when she'd been huddled against the door on the drive out here.

"It'll be okay," he whispered to her as he brought his hand down.

"I'm fine," she said.

He nodded with a slight smile. "I know."

Wade had never kissed a suspect, but he would have done it now if he hadn't thought it would make Jasmine cry even more. She was barely hanging on, and he needed to leave her with her dignity.

"I'll be parked at the end of Elmer's lane if you need me," Wade said as he stepped back from the door. Snow was falling in earnest now, but in his trunk he had a heavy sleeping bag that he used on stakeouts like this. "I'll come to the door in the morning, before I go over to my grandfather's."

"You can't sleep outside all night. It's freezing out here. I'll leave the kitchen door unlocked in case you need to come inside."

"Don't leave anything unlocked. I'll duck into the barn if I need to."

Jasmine nodded.

Wade watched her walk to the kitchen door and go inside the house. Only then did he head back to the driver's door. He wondered if he'd get any sleep tonight. He was losing his edge. The next thing he knew, he was going to be offering pillows to everyone he arrested and wishing them sweet dreams. When had he turned into a soft touch?

He waited for the light to go out in the kitchen before he started his drive down the lane. He already felt lonely.

* * * * *

*Will Jasmine give Wade reason to
call Dry Creek home again?
Find out in
SILENT NIGHT IN DRY CREEK
by Janet Tronstad.
Available in October 2009
from Love Inspired®*

For private investigator
Wade Sutton, Dry Creek
holds too many memories—
and none of them fond.
Yet he can't say no when
the sheriff asks him to
watch over a woman
who might be in danger.
Getting to know lovely
Jasmine Hunter just might
give Wade a good reason
to call Dry Creek home
once more….

Look for
Silent Night in Dry Creek
by
Janet Tronstad

*Available October
wherever books are sold.*

Steeple
Hill®

LI87553

REQUEST YOUR FREE BOOKS!

2 FREE RIVETING INSPIRATIONAL NOVELS
PLUS 2 FREE MYSTERY GIFTS

Love Inspired®
SUSPENSE

YES! Please send me 2 FREE Love Inspired® Suspense novels and my 2 FREE mystery gifts (gifts are worth about $10). After receiving them, if I don't wish to receive any more books, I can return the shipping statement marked "cancel". If I don't cancel, I will receive 4 brand-new novels every month and be billed just $4.24 per book in the U.S. or $4.74 per book in Canada. That's a savings of over 20% off the cover price. It's quite a bargain! Shipping and handling is just 50¢ per book.* I understand that accepting the 2 free books and gifts places me under no obligation to buy anything. I can always return a shipment and cancel at any time. Even if I never buy another book, the two free books and gifts are mine to keep forever.

123 IDN EYM2 323 IDN EYNE

Name	(PLEASE PRINT)

Address	Apt. #

City	State/Prov.	Zip/Postal Code

Signature (if under 18, a parent or guardian must sign)

Mail to Steeple Hill Reader Service:

IN U.S.A.: P.O. Box 1867, Buffalo, NY 14240-1867
IN CANADA: P.O. Box 609, Fort Erie, Ontario L2A 5X3

Not valid to current subscribers of Love Inspired Suspense books.

Want to try two free books from another series?
Call 1-800-873-8635 or visit www.morefreebooks.com

* Terms and prices subject to change without notice. Prices do not include applicable taxes. Sales tax applicable in N.Y. Canadian residents will be charged applicable provincial taxes and GST. Offer not valid in Quebec. This offer is limited to one order per household. All orders subject to approval. Credit or debit balances in a customer's account(s) may be offset by any other outstanding balance owed by or to the customer. Please allow 4 to 6 weeks for delivery. Offer available while quantities last.

Your Privacy: Steeple Hill Books is committed to protecting your privacy. Our Privacy Policy is available online at www.SteepleHill.com or upon request from the Reader Service. From time to time we make our lists of customers available to reputable third parties who may have a product or service of interest to you. If you would prefer we not share your name and address, please check here. ☐

LISUS09

Love Inspired
SUSPENSE

TITLES AVAILABLE NEXT MONTH

Available October 13, 2009

HEARTS IN THE CROSSHAIRS by Susan Page Davis

She came to be inaugurated—and left dodging bullets. Dave Hutchins of Maine's Executive Protection Unit doesn't know who wants to kill governor Jillian Goff. Still, he won't let her get hurt on his watch, not even when he finds his own heart getting caught in the crosshairs.

GUARDED SECRETS by Leann Harris

"If I die, it won't be an accident." Lilly Burkstrom can't forget her ex-husband's words...especially after his "accidental" death. As her fear builds, the only person this single mother can trust is Detective Jonathan Littledeer. Can he keep Lilly safe?

TRIAL BY FIRE by Cara Putman

Her mother's house was first. Then her brother's. County prosecutor Tricia Jamison is sure she's next on the arsonist's list. But who is after her family? And why does every fire throw her in the path of Noah Brust, the firefighter who can't forgive or forget their shared past?

DÉJÀ VU by Jenness Walker

Cole Leighton can barely believe it when a woman on his bus is abducted—in an *exact* reflection of a scene from the bestseller he's reading. Someone's bringing the book to life... and Kenzie Jacobs is trapped in the grisly story. Now the killer is writing his own ending, and none of the twists and turns lead to happily ever after.

LISCNMBPA0909